Asterats And Other Stories

E. S. Martell

Second Initiative Press

AsteRats And Other Stories

Copyright © 2017 by Eric S. Martell

Visit the author's website at www.ericmartellauthor.com

Cover Art by Eric Martell

Second Initiative Press

5831 Wilson Road

Venice, Florida, USA 34293-6885

Printed in the USA

ISBN: 978-1-948063-48-7 EPub

ISBN: 978-0-9989805-5-3 Paperback

Vox audita perit littera scripta manet.

Contents

LIFE, SPACE, AND IMAGINATION

From the inside of a computer to the surface of the Earth. From a tortured mind to the depths of space. From suburbia to city high-rise. There is no escape.

This anthology brings you stories to stretch your imagination; stories that will leave you wondering.

This collection is the perfect introduction to the work of E. S. Martell and is a great companion piece to his longer novels.

One Candle From Dark

*W*ho isn't fascinated by the idea of the Apocalypse? The Carrington Event in 1859 involved a solar flare that was so powerful, it destroyed telegraph equipment all over the globe. If such an event happened today, it's been estimated that nine out of ten people would be dead within the year. The survivors might not be so lucky either. Here's an example:

She'd been angry when Tom bought the case of candles. Each one of the thin white tapers seemed a nail in the coffin of their slowly dying marriage. At first, she'd thought his penchant for storing emergency supplies was cute, but then, when money became scarce, it had seemed stupid and paranoid. Now she was glad that she had the candles. They kept the ghosts at bay.

All of the supplies were running low. It was only a matter of time before the little lights were gone and the ghosts would get her.

The wind was starting to pick up. Jane stood on her front porch and looked at the dark southern sky. A storm was coming. From the darkness and the flickering lightning, it was going to be a serious one. Perhaps it would cool things off. It had been unseasonably hot since the flash.

She glanced over her shoulder into the darkened house. The lace curtains in the kitchen were blowing in the wind coming through the screen. It blew in strong gusts every day but gradually died down as evening progressed, leaving the nights to swelter in the unusual heat.

She entered the house, bypassing the kitchen, taking one slow step at a time, glancing at the dark corners. She wearily trudged up the stairs to the master bedroom. There she looked out the window, down at the distant road.

She thought about lighting a candle. She'd always hated the dark and now that the ghosts were here, she hated it even more. It was winning. The blackness would eventually conquer everything. As far as she knew, she was the sole point of light left in the world. She looked at the candle box for a moment.

Returning her attention to the south, she sighed deeply and hoped no one would start up the long driveway toward her house. The area behind the barn wasn't a place she wanted to visit again, but she knew she'd have to go back there eventually.

Tom had gone off to work as usual on the last normal day. He drove over to the Cummins' house to pick up George. The two men worked at an aircraft plant almost one hundred miles away. That was the best employment available near the lightly populated, rural area. The commute had seemed worthwhile, given their debts and reduced income.

Jane had watched Tom drive down the hill from their house. She had seen George climb in from where he'd been standing by his mailbox. The pickup had turned onto the main road trailing a cloud of dust and vanished. She'd gone about her daily chores, feeding the chickens, gathering eggs, and then tending to the garden behind the house.

The garden was Jane's primary interest. The vegetables were thriving, even though it was still early in the year. Now that the unseasonable weather had set in, it seemed like the corn shot up inches every day. It wouldn't be long before the ears were ripening. She'd never seen as productive a growing season. Maybe it was the heat. The sun seemed brighter, somehow.

She'd been bent over, weeding the potatoes, when the flash happened. She wasn't sure what had occurred, just that it suddenly grew brighter. She straightened and looked around, puzzled. It was almost like the sun had been shaded by some high clouds that had suddenly disappeared. She shrugged, then turned to the house. It was time for a break, and she was thirsty.

The lights wouldn't come on it the kitchen. Irritated, she checked the other rooms. It looked like the power was out. The stupid electric company couldn't seem to keep the service going. It went off at irregular periods, and she was used to that. It'd come on eventually.

Jane continued working on her chores until lunchtime. She threw some greens to the chickens, checked on the two goats, and worked some more in the garden.

The power still wasn't on when she went in for lunch, so she made herself a ham sandwich, closing the refrigerator door quickly to conserve the small amount of cold that was still in the machine. If the power didn't come on soon, she'd start to lose food. That irritated her, and so did the fact that the phone was out. She couldn't even call to report an outage.

At two pm, as on every weekday, she walked down the hill to check the mail. The box at the end of the mile-long drive was empty. Either the mail carrier hadn't come, or there was no mail for them today. That made her happy. Most days the thought of the bills waiting in the mailbox was depressing. The absence of mail was pleasant, and the long journey back up the hill to the house seemed easier as a result.

Tom was due home by eight. She hated the dark house and the dark corners of the rooms, but it would be better when he returned unless they started fighting again. The arguments were wearing her out. No, the arguments were erasing their love; that was what was happening. Their discord was slowly putting out the light in her life.

She'd lit a candle as dusk gradually morphed into night. She was beginning to worry since he still hadn't arrived.

She tried to dial his number, but the cell system was down, or perhaps her phone wasn't working correctly. It was off, and she couldn't get it to start. She thought about charging it, but the power was still off.

It was a long, hot night. The wind had died, and the still air held more heat than was usual for this time of year. She tossed fitfully on top of the sheets in their second-floor bedroom. Tom's absence made her nervous. Their relationship had been deteriorating for months due to the financial stress when she'd lost her job, but she still relied on his presence. Something about his quiet competence made her feel secure.

He wasn't back by morning. Jane was forced to consider the idea that he might have had an accident. She had some cereal for breakfast. Might as well use up the milk before it went bad. The refrigerator was now no more than a storage cabinet. She cleaned out the spoiling food, shaking her head at the waste.

Somewhere Tom had a solar-powered radio. That might help with her isolation. She dug around in the spare room upstairs. That was where he kept the bulk of their emergency supplies. Eventually, she found the radio. It was still in the original packaging, hidden from view behind some boxes of ammunition.

The sun was shining brightly and the radio powered up quickly, but there was nothing to receive. Turning up the volume only resulted in static. There weren't any stations broadcasting. She couldn't find anything from one end of the dial to the other. She went back inside and sat at the kitchen table, her head in her hands.

She watched the wind blow the lace curtains, her mind blank. After a time, there was a faint noise. She could hear a shrill screaming blowing up the hill, carried on the wind. She laboriously climbed to her feet and looked out the window.

The sound was coming from the Cummins' house across the road. It shouldn't have carried to her, but some trick of the wind seemed to waft it into her kitchen. Jane scrounged around for her binoculars. She used those for bird watching, but now they seemed perfect for spying on her neighbors.

She couldn't clearly see what was going on. Their house was too far for that, but she could see that it was on fire. Smoke was carried down the wind at an increasing rate. The fire seemed to be out of control.

She stiffened attentively as two figures came out of the house and trotted down the sidewalk. As they walked away, Mary Cummins came out of the house, stumbling across the porch. One of the figures turned back and raised something in its hand.

Jane heard a shot. Mary Cummins tumbled forward off the porch, rolling down the steps in a flurry of arms and legs, to land, unmoving, on the front walk. The two figures turned and continued toward the road.

Jane watched for a moment, trying to hold the binoculars steady, although her hands were shaking. The next obvious target for the two marauders was her house. They were coming directly toward her drive. She was ready to panic, but then she found a degree of control in the thought that the two were on foot, and it would take them several minutes to get to her door. She dropped the binoculars and dashed for the gun case.

That was another thing that she and Tom had fought over. He owned more firearms than she felt necessary or even prudent. Now she was glad that he'd forced her to learn to shoot the light hunting rifle. She could manage its smaller caliber, and it had a good telescopic sight. She located the gun, fumbled for some cartridges, and loaded the magazine.

It took three attempts for her shaking hands to insert the magazine into the well on the bottom of the weapon, but it finally clicked in. She released the bolt lock. The mechanism slammed shut with a solid, metallic sound, carrying a cartridge into the chamber. The rifle was ready. Was she?

She hesitated, looking at the front door, then climbed the stairs and went into their bedroom. The window overlooked the long drive that ascended the hill. The two marauders – she could now see that they were men – were about halfway up. She watched, waiting for them to get closer.

There was a fence about a hundred yards from the house where the driveway gate hung open. The men approached the gate and Jane aimed through the telescopic sight, observing them. Both carried handguns, but she couldn't make out the weapons' details. One was also carrying a large bag filled with some items that must have belonged to the Cummins family. They gestured toward her house and joked back and forth. She could hear their laughter faintly.

One lagged behind to check his pistol. He chambered a round as the two came through the gate. Jane shot him before he could take another step, then instantly aimed at the other man. He hadn't heard the shot or noticed that his compatriot had fallen. The wind was gusting hard and had kept much of the sound confined inside the bedroom. She aimed at the center of his chest. Her mind was cold and elsewhere as she pulled the trigger. The rifle bucked against her shoulder, and the man went down.

He wasn't dead, though. He writhed around on the ground and fired several shots at the house. None came close to her window, although she heard a downstairs windows shatter. She aimed, took a deep breath, and fired again. The writhing man stopped moving and dropped the pistol.

Jane carried the rifle with her as she went down the drive to check on the two. Tears were streaming down her cheeks, and she could barely walk. Her face was pale with shock as she bent over the bodies. The bag, a pillowcase, contained some collectible items that she recognized as belonging to Mary Cummins.

She took the two handguns and the pillowcase of stolen possessions into the house. Then she returned to the corpses, pushing her two-wheeled garden cart. It had an oversized flatbed. Its long handles and bicycle wheels provided extra leverage that allowed her to move both bodies to the back of the barn.

She couldn't leave them on the drive. How would Tom get in, and what would he think?

At some subconscious level, she feared that they would begin to stink and the wind would blow the odor into the house. She couldn't stay there with that kind of smell.

It was a hard job, but she eventually dumped the second body and returned the cart to the garden. She was still in shock, but now she moved deliberately, calmly, as she went into the kitchen and fixed herself a glass of iced tea, without the ice, of course.

Jane sat at the kitchen table. The tea glass was empty. She had placed the men's two handguns on the other end of the table after cursorily examining them. One – the revolver – held two fired cartridges. She had only heard the shot that had dropped Mary. The only other person in the Cummins house had been Mary's aged mother.

Jane did not want to go over there to check. Mary's body still lay at the foot of the steps. Somehow Jane was sure that Mary's mother lay dead somewhere in the depths of the smoldering house.

It was time to think. Something had happened. Something terrible. The power had gone off; then Tom hadn't come home. Her phone and radio didn't work. The Cummins were dead, and she had two corpses rotting in the heat behind the barn. Everything was somehow related. It had begun when she was working in the garden.

Now she remembered. The sun had flashed. That seemed to be the start of things. She'd noticed the power was off right after that.

Tom had gone through various catastrophic events with her, arguing that they should prepare themselves for anything. She wondered if the flash had been a solar flare. They'd talked about that possibility. The power and electronics must be related to that. If that was the cause, it was no wonder that Tom wasn't back. His car must have died, and he'd now be on foot trying to walk almost ninety miles to get back home.

She calculated that if he managed to make twenty miles a day, he'd be back by Monday. She resolved to be ready when he returned. She'd show him that she now understood and appreciated his efforts to be prepared.

Jane had brought all of the rifle ammunition into the bedroom. She had set up a shooting position with a blanket to kneel on and a padded rest on the window sill. One of the dead men's handguns, a revolver, was securely belted to her waist. Now she kept watch for more marauders.

If the problem had been a solar flare, then no one would be driving. Newer cars and trucks wouldn't work, and people wouldn't be able to pump gas without electricity.

There were two smaller towns within a day's walking distance. Those places held many people who would want the supplies that were in her house. She was prepared to defend herself and her possessions until Tom got back. He would know better what to do, and he would take over. She'd show him that she understood and he'd be proud of her. Their fights would be a thing of the past.

Night fell uneventfully. No one else had shown up, either on the road or coming up her drive. The wind had started to diminish but was still blowing harder than usual for nighttime. The curtains billowed softly in the wind and an eerie feeling permeated the house. Jane found herself continuously looking over her shoulders and peering fearfully into the dark corners of the rooms. There was an invisible presence that demanded her attention.

She moved from room to room, pausing uneasily at each door to stare into the dark, trying to see if there was someone or something there. The revolver in her hand did not provide any solace. Her sense of unease was too agitating and yet too diffuse for her to locate the source.

She suddenly remembered the candles. A few minutes later, she had placed two lighted candles in each room, leaving only her bedroom dark. She had shut the windows and pulled the curtains so that the flame wouldn't be visible down on the road. It would draw no unwanted attention. She'd sit in the dark bedroom, where she could watch the drive, unobserved from below.

Something about the candles seemed to keep the spooky presence at a distance, but she could still sense the unease.

She first thought that it was the ghost of Mary Cummins or her old mother. She slowly became convinced it was the two men she had shot without warning. She thought, no, she knew they wanted revenge for their deaths.

She tried to convince herself that they had deserved to die. They'd killed the women across the street, after all.

Somehow that rationale didn't make her feel better. Their spirits were still present, hovering around in some dark, unknown space, demanding revenge. The candles were all that kept them from reaching her.

Morning found her asleep at the window. The candles had burned down. She had replaced them every couple of hours throughout the night, but now their remains were pools of wax, accompanied by a slightly smoky odor in each room.

Jane awoke with a start. There was a small group of people walking up the drive toward the house.

They'd already passed the gate and now were only about fifty yards away. There were three men and two women. All held a weapon of some form. One man had an ax, another a long length of steel bar. The third, a long gun. Both of the women carried kitchen knives.

They gave off a combination of guilty furtiveness and brazen, unconcerned boldness, as if they knew they shouldn't be planning on looting her house, but were determined to do it despite that knowledge and weren't worried about being caught in the act.

The rifle spoke five times. After observing the scene to make sure no one else was coming, Jane went for the garden cart. Two hours later five more bodies were beginning to bloat in the heat behind the barn.

That night the ghosts were back in force. All seven of the unknown looters were after her. The candles were the only defense. She lit them in every room, then cooked one of Tom's packaged emergency meals on the portable camp stove. The angry, spiritual presence seemed to move around and around the outside of the house as she ate.

Later, she watched at the window, leaving only to check candles and replace those that had burned out. The wind continued to blow. It hadn't cooled off. The night was hot, and she missed the air conditioning. They hadn't been running it much since it was too expensive. Having a break from the heat would be nice. Maybe Tom could figure out how to get it going again when he returned.

In the morning she drew some water from the old cistern and took a most welcome bath. The water was almost the same temperature as the air, but it cooled as it evaporated from her skin, leaving her feeling somewhat refreshed.

Breakfast was more dehydrated food. The food buckets held a variety of meals, and Jane eagerly went through them, organizing them into piles so that she could eat for a week without any duplication.

She looked out the kitchen window. Things looked wrong out in the yard. Feathers were blowing across the grass. Something had gotten at the chickens during the night. Jane hadn't heard it. The chicken run was behind the house, and the wind had blown the noise away. Either that or perhaps she had slept. She didn't know.

The chickens were all dead. They'd been savaged. Feathers and blood were everywhere. Jane feared the ghosts had gotten them until she saw a large dog's paw print outlined in blood on the back step. She hurried to the small barn to check the goats. The scene there was the same. Both Billy and Nan had their throats ripped out. Something had partially devoured both goats' abdomens.

Jane backed away in horror, staring at the violent scene. It somehow bothered her more than the bodies of the people she'd shot. She reached behind her for the barn door, fumbling for it as she tried to step out, her gaze still fixed on the two goats. They'd been her special pets. Now they were bloody messes; nastily dead.

There was a growl from behind her. She whirled to face two huge dogs moving slowly toward her, jaws gaping, slaver dripping to the ground. She raised the revolver and fired. The ground between the dogs puffed with the shot, but the animals only flinched, then continued to advance.

Jane ducked back inside and started to shut the door. The dogs lunged forward with snarls, wedging themselves in the narrow opening. Jane shot again and again until the revolver clicked futilely.

One dog was dead. The other was struggling. It limped slowly away from the door, then dropped to its stomach and crawled a few feet farther before becoming still.

She looked at the sides of the barn, the corners of the house, and around the yard. Nothing. She started for the house.

About halfway to the door, she heard a rush and a chorus of growls over the wind's noise. A whole pack of dogs was coming around the far corner of the barn, running full-out towards her. She screamed and ran.

The distance to the back door seemed infinite, but she somehow moved closer, her heart pounding in her chest. She didn't look back. It would only slow her down.

A yank at the doorknob and a spin followed by a slam, then the door shuddered as several heavy bodies impacted it. She was afraid the frame would break. The dogs snarled and clawed on the wood outside.

She pulled the portable island to the door, overturning it, so the solid top was against the bottom panel. That additional barrier made her feel more secure until she remembered the front door. It was open, the entrance to the house barred only by the flimsy screen.

She sprinted through the rooms, nearly falling as the parlor rug slid across the polished wood under her feet. The front door! She slammed it and turned the deadbolt.

There was a movement. A dog was looking through the sidelight window at her. Where was her rifle?

She flew up the stairs to the master bedroom. The wind had blown the door closed. The ghosts were conspiring to keep her out. She fumbled with the doorknob as a window shattered downstairs. There was the scrabble of rapidly moving claws on the wood floor and the heavy thump of a body falling as its feet slid out from under it at the sharp corner to the stairs.

The knob yielded, and she slammed the bedroom door before the animal cleared the top of the staircase. She lunged for the bed, hands reaching for her weapon. She cried out as her hands touched the polished wood of the stock.

With the comforting weight cradled in her arms, she considered what to do, ignoring the scratching and growling on the landing.

Jane climbed through the window onto the porch roof and attracted the dogs by yelling.

They clustered in a constantly moving pack below her, dancing in their eagerness. Even the one inside burst out again, as they howled and barked, clamoring for her flesh. The rifle spoke multiple times. The yard became silent.

By the time she'd wheeled the bodies to the back of the barn, it was growing dark again. She'd paused to eat and perhaps drifted away into what must have been a fugue state. She wasn't sure where the hours had gone. Her emotions seemed flat, almost dead. She felt numb.

The ghosts were thick around the house in the dark, trying to come through the windows. The candlelight held them at bay. Now they moaned for vengeance and howled with a hunger for her body. She shuddered as she kept her vigil at the bedroom window.

Two more men tried the drive the next day. Their bodies went into the rotting pile of flesh that was making a nauseating stench behind the barn. Jane didn't know if she'd be able to go back there again. It was lucky that the wind blew the smell away from the house. She thought of it as a dark cloud that made her retch.

It was evening when another marauder started up the driveway. He limped towards the house, moving slowly. She inspected the man through the telescopic sight. This one had disguised himself with a blood-stained rag wrapped around his head, covering part of his face. She sighed, willing him to turn back.

He paused. She hoped he'd change his mind and leave.

The ghosts, now bolder, whirled around him and drove him onward. Jane choked back a sob. She was tired of killing. Maybe it would be better just to submit. If she were dead, she could join the ghosts, and not have to worry about fighting them. If she were a ghost, she could fly around the outside of the house in the dark and not worry about anything but the candles.

Those would be gone soon anyhow. Jane had been burning so many every night that the case was nearly empty. When their little lights were gone, the ghosts would surely enter the house and get her. The thought of being absorbed into their black cloud of stench terrified her.

Down on the drive, the figure came on toward the house. Jane steeled her will. If only Tom were home, he'd know what to do about the ghosts and everything else. His calm presence would make her feel secure. Gone were her doubts in him. The carefully stored supplies that once seemed crazy were now the work of a sane and prudent man. She wanted him back.

The figure below came on, one limping step after another. The Marauder was carrying a large corn knife, a type of machete. Jane could see blood on the square end of the weapon. Had it been used to kill some other hapless woman? The man kept coming.

In due course, the rifle kicked against her shoulder, and the body dropped by the gate. She descended to get the now blood-stained garden cart. The ghosts were becoming bolder in the gathering dusk. They were howling on the wind, the hot wind.

She dragged the body onto the cart and started for the back of the barn, only to pause. The rag about the man's head had caught in one of the wheels and had wound around the axle. She tugged at it, and it slipped off his head.

It was Tom.

She might have screamed in horror, or perhaps she mutely smiled in despairing acceptance of the death of her hope. She didn't know. Her mind had snapped to a featureless white, then had gone completely blank.

When she came back into herself a little, she looked at him. He had been cut across the forehead; a jagged slash that extended down across and deep into his right eye, blinding him on that side. The purpose of the rag hadn't been to disguise but to bandage. She saw that, and also noted that her shot, as usual, had been dead center in his chest.

She didn't remember moving his body. When she eventually found herself in the kitchen, she thought to look out the window. His body was gone, and the garden cart was standing on the front walk, fresh blood dripping to the flagstones below.

She was getting sloppy. She'd have to move it, but maybe tomorrow. Right now she had a more pressing problem. The ghosts were back, louder than ever, whirling around the house in the dusk.

She lit a candle, carrying it with her through the dimly lit rooms.

She was running out of candles to fight the dark. The ghosts were more powerful than ever. She could hear Tom's voice mixed in with their continual plaints. They wouldn't wait. They demanded retribution. She wandered aimlessly from room to room, unaware that the hot wax from the candle sometimes dripped on her hand.

She found the way back into her mind when the candle burned out. She was sitting in the master bedroom by the window. She picked some wax off the back of her hand, calmly touching the little blisters it had raised.

Jane did not know how long she sat in the darkening house. The ghosts were spinning through the wind outside, triumphant cries in their silent voices. The rest of the house was dark. Her bedroom was lighted by the next to the last candle. Now, it had almost burned out.

With shaking hands, she took the final candle and held its wick to the barely flickering flame. It caught, flared, then steadied, bringing a comforting light to the room. The ghosts gave cries of disappointment and moved away from the opened window.

They had forever; they could afford to wait. Their dark was winning. She'd been so sure that she was of the light, a creature of life and hope. The ghosts argued otherwise. Perhaps they were correct.

Jane carefully stuck the base of the last candle in the candle holder, then sat quite still, her hands in her lap. She had to make a decision. She'd make it by the time the candle was gone.

A single rifle cartridge sat on the window sill in front of her. She could keep on fighting, or she could give up. The ghosts were waiting for her just outside. She could hear Tom's voice somewhere out there, calling her name. It sounded as though he was slowly coming closer in the dark.

The ghosts cried expectantly outside, not loudly, but never quite still. She took a shallow breath and looked at the candle, then a deeper breath, and looked at the rifle cartridge.

She was just one candle from dark.

The End

Blue Streamers

The antecedent for this story is unusual. I had the unpleasant experience of having to have open-heart surgery quite a number of years ago. This was due to a genetic defect that predisposed me to suffer from atrial fibrillation. During my recovery period, I was given narcotics and after three days on some pretty powerful pills, I saw the characters in this story as clearly as if I were reading about them in a book. I suppose you could say that I was hallucinating, but perhaps, just perhaps, I was actually tuning into another reality somewhere.

Breaker paused at the drop-off point. He stood inches away from the edge overlooking the five-kilometer drop to the valley below, poised for a moment as if he were about to leap over the edge; then he spun to look at the brotherhood hall.

It was a long, low building with massive timbers supporting the flat flagstones that made up the roof. The timbered walls were broken at intervals by massive rock columns, giving the entire structure the appearance of something that had survived for centuries, but which was gradually being crushed into the ground by its constant weight of snow. There was a large, flagstone patio that fronted the building. This was the site of all social activity and also the place where the clan linked arms in the face of the worst gales to perform the traditional midwinter storm-defiance roars.

The poles at the doors were covered with streamers of ribbon, snapping and popping in the stiff wind that roared down the slope. The fabric was woven of fine thread, so tough that the cloth was almost wear-proof, nevertheless the older streamers were frayed and tattered by the wind, as well as bleached nearly white. The newer ones were a deep, rich, and shiny blue.

The color stood for valor and was the exact shade of newly-spilled blood.

Valor, tradition, self-reliance, brotherhood, and family were on Breaker's mind. He was young and had his name to make and honor to protect, so these thoughts were entirely appropriate for him as he faced the gusting wind.

Breaker gloried in the fact that the wind was nearly gale-force. He pushed his massive head forward, defying it to shove him off the cliff. The wind responded by whipping his long hair and beard into his eyes.

A season ago, he would not have been able to stand in such a strong gust, let alone at the edge of a precipice. The past winter had been a long one, and he had used the time well, eating and growing strong. This year was his first as an adult, and he was just coming into the first flush of his power and mass.

Now others of the tightly knit community came forth, laughing and calling to each other in deep voices that blended in the wind into a roaring sound. They were a formidable clan in their massed strength.

A flock of ice birds came whirling by on the gusting wind. Breaker took two quick steps and leaped high to catch one in his mouth. The wind gusted and blew him backward dangerously close to the edge. His brothers roared in approval. He crunched the delicate, cold body, relishing the taste.

This was life! The struggle to survive. The strength that conquered the elements! The strength that conquered the competition! He knew deep in his hearts that he was ready.

The echo of the massed onlooker's roar bounced down the valley, rebounding from peak to peak and fading into untold distances. After a time, an answering set of bellows came from the other fraternal groups that were gathered to greet the day, each in front of their clan halls, scattered among the peaks.

Breaker could almost make out individual voices in the chorus. Long study ensured that he recognized his competitors.

His clan moved closer, and they came together in a tight bunch, jostling for position as each tried to increase his status by moving closer to the leading males. Breaker alone stood slightly apart. This was not because it was expected of a young male before his coming of age, but because he fully understood the status game and knew he was not yet ready to compete with the older and heavier members. Some of them were over twice his mass and could easily shove him back.

Instead, his intelligence prompted him to stand aloof, as if he had no need to compete for status. He had concluded that this worked to his benefit in that the others recognized it as a form of superiority.

In fact, several of them glanced curiously at him as they attempted to work their way into the center of the scrum. Breaker's gain in status was confirmed when two of the younger males made their way over and stood near him, electing to bathe in his glory, small though it was.

After a short time, Stoneskull, their leader, and most massive male, shouted that it was time to gather fuel and the milling group gradually became organized into several queues which made their way upward past the brotherhood hall and spread out along the edge of the dark, encroaching forest that overshadowed their ledge.

The forest was composed of flither trees nearly as old as the stones. It held numerous dangers and was nearly impassible. The only way through was to work along the edge of one of the many avalanche paths that cut through the foreboding mass of trees.

Strong though the trees were, the massed snow, shooting down at high velocity from the mountainside above snapped the trunks from the rocks and tossed them around like broken matchsticks. This was a good thing, as far as Breaker was concerned. Not only did it provide an easy source of firewood, but it also allowed easy egress from the brotherhood's steading. Worming through the tightly packed flither trees left one unable to guard against even the lesser predators that roamed the woods.

The groups gathered broken wood, vying to see who could bring the largest piece back to the pile on the front patio. The task was finished by late morning. Stoneskull allowed them to relax until mid-day feeding time.

Clatter came up to Breaker ostensibly to engage in conversation. This was something that Breaker usually tried to avoid, since Clatter was a lightweight, not to be taken seriously. Still, his words were cunning and often held two or three meanings, so Breaker did not actively shun him.

"Breaker, your tree piece was one of the largest today," the thinner male said. "You've put on a lot of strength over the winter. It is apparent to all of us that this is your time. Have you given any thought to choosing?" Then without giving Breaker time to consider, he added, "You'd better have because others are already making plans."

Breaker traced Clatter's glance and saw Heaver standing in the middle of an admiring group of younger males.

He snorted and shook his head making his hair and beard fly, then said, "I've been busy working. What boots it to make such plans? 'Tis well known that the shes have their own way at the choosing ritual. Besides, who among us has made the descent this spring? No one knows which girl will present herself until we go down and see. Even the older, married males have yet to descend to greet their mid-winter born children."

Clatter shrugged and went over to Heaver's group, doubtless to instill some germ of conflict there.

Breaker felt ill-used. Reminding him of Heaver was not a friendly thing for Clatter to have done. There was bad blood between the two of them. Heaver's Pere, Lifter, had taken Breaker's Mere to wife after Breaker's Pere had fallen from a high ledge. Taking a widow as a wife was an uncommon action, but marginally acceptable. However, it drove an unmovable wedge between Breaker and his Mere and also led to Heaver's antagonism.

No one had seen the accident. Falls were certainly common enough. Group members often slipped and fell, sometimes with minor result and others times fatally. However, Breaker held a deep suspicion that Heaver and his Pere, Lifter, held some culpability in the event. They had been on the same ledge as his sire at the time of the accident. This would have given them the opportunity to push someone who might have been unsuspecting.

Lifter was wifeless due to a prowling Greater Shait which had taken her as she returned from a late errand in the valley depths. He had been so quick to claim Breaker's Mere, once she was widowed, that it was unseemly.

Breaker tried to put the entire situation out of his mind by tussling with some of the others, but his energy level was too much for them, and they backed off, refusing contact. It was true. This was his year, his season was upon him, and his hormones were raging through his body. His muscles felt like bands of metal as a result.

He sat on a rock to think. If it was not forthcoming without his solicitation, he would ask Stoneskull for permission to descend. There was no way that the elder could deny him the right to make the journey. He was mentally and physically prepared for the hardship he would encounter, and he had already forged a courtship dagger in secret. Some of the males made a big thing out of creating the little knives, but he had preferred to work alone and privately at a forge of his own creation.

His courtship dagger was an ornate and lightweight work of art that appeared heavier than it was. He had already procured the mass of thin streamers that would be tied to the hilt. Their drag through the thicker air deep in the valley would ensure that the dagger would do no major damage to the maid who received the falling blade.

At mid-day feeding, Breaker was not surprised when Stoneskull called his name along with half a dozen others, including Heaver.

The leader stood and spoke with his deep, gusty voice.

"Young males. This spring you have come into your season. It's been obvious to all of us, despite your reticence in showing it."

There was a baaing of laughter from the entire group. Breaker and his cohort could no more suppress their boisterousness than they could stop breathing. Everyone knew which of the group was full of strange urges brought on by the onset of spring.

Stoneskull continued. "Although we will miss your help, you are hereby excused from your duties so that you can journey to the village of the shes. Take care to carry provisions. Even though spring is here, it is not unusual for a late blizzard to make the descent hazardous. Three years ago one such snowstorm killed all of the seekers. We cannot afford to lose an entire group in that manner. It weakens the brotherhood and makes it difficult for us all to survive."

Breaker shrugged mentally. Everyone knew of the event. The blizzard had been days in coming. All knew it was on the way, yet the foolish ones had started their descent out of fear that the best shes would already have chosen mates from the competing clans. Their death was their fault. He would be more careful, of course. Besides, the weather promised fair for the next several days. There was no sign of snow in the wind.

The massive leader said, "Gather what you need from the common supplies. Take care to avoid predators. Climb carefully and do not slip. Trust no one from another clan and only trust those from your clan lightly. The journey is a time of anarchy. Normal rules do not apply. Still, take note! I will not hear of dire deeds among your group. If one of you kills another member of our clan, he will meet me in combat upon his return. Now go!"

There was a roar as the entire assembly repeated, "Go!"

Breaker and the others ran to gather the supplies they would need.

The other candidates were closely aligned with Heaver due to his constant flattery. They had conspired to block Breaker's way, giving his chief rival time to select. Heaver had already appropriated the best blanket and the best kukuri by the time Breaker shouldered his way through the door, pushing some of the lighter males aside.

Breaker said nothing, only selecting items he deemed were adequate. He ignored Heaver's taunting leer and gathered his supplies in silence. When he was ready, he exited the hall and headed for the edge.

Stoneskull met him there, at the drop-off.

"Breaker, take care on the way. Your father was my closest friend, and I wish not to hear of your falling as did he. You might not know it, but you have enemies who wish the worst for you. Journey well and come back a full male," he said.

Breaker nodded silently, then turned and made the first leap, dropping down the vertical cliff face to a ledge which extended horizontally to a passable crack leading downward.

His thoughts turned, as they inevitably must, to the season. It was spring, and he was on his way to seek a mate. He hoped that he would be successful and find a girl who was the envy of the others.

A loose rock rapped on the wall beside him, spinning past and receding into the depths below. He looked upward to see Heaver staring down. Heaver called, "It was loose. I knocked it off to keep the others safe. I did not see you there."

Breaker did not answer him. It was apparent that he'd been the target of an attack. He moved quickly along the ledge, then bypassed the crack he'd initially thought to follow, opting for the more difficult cliff beyond. The others were not as surefooted as he and would not be likely to follow where he led. He hoped to avoid any additional accidents by taking the harder path.

He knew that such perfidy could exist, but had difficulty in ascribing it to a clan member, even one as unlikable as Heaver. In Breaker's mind, everyone should be honorable. Loyalty to family and clan was paramount. Personal honor and responsibility were values instilled by the clan leaders and enforced by the harsh environment.

The descent was long and beyond anyone's ability to accomplish in the half-day that they had left. He moved by stages from one foothold to the next; from one ledge to a lower one. By the time dark was approaching, he had separated himself from the others by hundreds of meters. None of them could match his skill at climbing, and he gradually quit worrying about their ill will. This mental shift was helped by the sheer joy he felt in climbing.

At dusk, Breaker rounded a corner of the cliff and found a deep crack that led back into the rocks. It would provide admirable shelter for the night since the floor was composed of boulders that had fallen from above and jammed into a narrower part of the fissure.

He sniffed carefully. There was a bit of odor about the place that did not seem right.

Drawing his heavy-bladed kukuri, he advanced slowly, all senses alert. It was well that he held the chopping weapon high. He suddenly realized that the fissure was the home of a Lesser Shait. This creature was not as dire as the Greater form but was still capable of killing a lone brother.

He became aware of a shadow that moved slowly toward him. He stopped and backed a bit to give himself more elbow room. The Lesser Shait could mimic the rocks that surrounded it, blending into the background until it was nearly invisible. It continued stalking him as he backed up.

He picked up a heavy piece of stone to hold in his other hand. Shaits were difficult opponents -- all pointy parts, teeth, claws, and body spikes. Their body spikes were venomous as well, so it was not good to come into direct contact with them.

With a rustle, the predator moved quickly to attack. Breaker slammed the stone forward, striking the creature's visual patch, then chopped wildly with the kukuri. His blows severed several of the clawed arms. The Shait made a low moaning cry and lunged forward, trying to push him off the edge of the cliff.

Breaker slammed the stone against the creature again, then chopped downward with all his strength. The blade struck home, somehow severing a critical nerve plexus. The Shait curled into a ball form and ceased moving.

Breaker poked it carefully with the point of his blade. It did not move, so he slid between it and the wall, found a spot on the ball that was not protected with a spike, and shoved hard. The Shait rolled forward and started to fall over the edge.

It was good that he had been careful. It was not fully disabled. Sensing doom in the fall, the creature lashed out and struck Breaker's leg with one of its claws. It tottered there, balanced on the edge, for a moment, then fell silently into the void.

Breaker sat down heavily, dismayed. His leg was already numb. Apparently, the venom was not limited to the body spikes as he'd heard. The claw strike, while minor, had disabled him.

He worked at the wound, finally parting his thick fur and opening the flesh with the kukuri to bleed the venom out. That offered some relief, and he gradually relaxed and fell asleep.

Morning found him sitting at the edge of the crevice, his leg throbbing, but no longer numb. As soon as it was light enough to see, he started downward. There was no time to heal. The sun was advancing in its cycle, and eligible shes would be as sensitive to its light as he. They would present themselves for courting whether he was there or not.

His leg slowed him and made the difficult path he'd chosen far more hazardous. He nearly fell several times before he decided to slow even more. Below, deep in the valley, he could see the rooftops of the village. This was the home of the shes and the younglings. The males of the brotherhood clans only descended to engage in the choosing and then to bring supplies to their mates. The shes never climbed as high as the males.

Breaker could see movement far below him off to the side along the more commonly used path. It looked like

Heaver and his friends were now well ahead. He sighed.
It couldn't be helped. The Lesser Shait had seen to that.
He'd have to go at his best speed and hope that he wasn't
too late.

His leg was aching by dusk, but he had reached the rim
wall above the village. This was the lookout where the
courting males laid up to observe the eligible maids as
they displayed themselves.

Breaker found a comfortable point and then carefully
studied the wall off to the left of his position. There was a
hint of movement about a fifth of the way around, and
he thought that might be Heaver's group. There was also
movement in three other places on the opposite side. His
clan was not the only one that had sent candidates. The
presence of the others meant that the possibility of
bloodshed was far higher.

Males would meet in challenge over a maid. Such
conflicts were all-out, no holds barred, and the loser was
usually thrown down the cliff to impress the shes. Breaker
stretched his leg and tried to get as comfortable as he
could. The morning was going to be interesting.

About mid-morning of the next day, some of the first
maidens sauntered forth. They wore gaily-colored
clothing and ribbons of various colors although none
were blue. That color was reserved for the males.

The males had positioned themselves along the rim wall
where they could be seen easily, each being careful to

stand in a manner that emphasized their desirableness. Breaker was content to sit and watch the drama. None of the maids seemed to him to meet his requirements.

The maids appeared not to notice, but Breaker assumed they were discretely assessing the candidates. The maidens clustered well away from the wall, but finally, two of them walked away from the group. These two seemed to be conversing and unaware of the males above. They gradually wandered closer to the rim wall.

Tension rippled over the males above. One of the two seemed to have become interested in snow flowers that were almost directly below a single male. When she came within range, he threw his courtship dagger in a high arc, ribbons streaming behind it. It came down point foremost, and she looked up, eyes tracking it carefully. Just when it seemed the knife would miss her, she stepped quickly forward and caught the ribbons, allowing the blade to nick the upper part of her bosom.

At the sight of the blood which flowed from her skin, the male above let out a great cry of triumph and began the descent to finalize his claim. The girl, carrying the knife, moved quickly to meet him.

There was an almost imperceptible increase in the tension above.

The second maid was a bit of a flirt. She moved close to several hopeful candidates but carefully stayed out of knife range. Finally, she got a bit too close, and one male threw his knife. It arched over and down, the maid studying it carefully. At the last moment, she turned her back and walked quickly away, allowing the knife to plunge point foremost into the rocky ground.

The disappointed male dropped out of sight. His only chance would be to retrieve the knife after dark and try again on the next day. If he were unsuccessful then, he would return to his clan in failure. Such individuals gradually became less and less social, finally retreating into the forests, there to live a solitary life as best they could or to become a predator's lunch. In either event, their names were struck off the roles of the brotherhood and never mentioned again.

———

Breaker continued to watch as several other maids came forth, caught the knives of their choices, and left to meet the happy males as they descended the cliff. He was disappointed. None of the girls in the valley seemed to fit his criteria.

A slight movement at the village gate drew his attention. A slim maid was standing there. Her hair was the exact color about which he'd dreamed. Her demeanor was a combination of shyness and bold assessment. She'd been watching the males on display from a hiding place and now was more actively assessing them. Breaker stood and showed himself immediately.

The movement caught her eye, and she looked directly at him. This was not normal behavior. It was not the best of form to look directly at a male. It usually portended a rejection, but Breaker moved his head, acknowledging her glance. She lifted her head, and his breath caught. She was beautiful, smaller than normal, but stunning in her grace, fur thickness, and color. He wanted her with all of his being.

She started moving in his direction, then paused. There was a rattle of stones from along the wall. Breaker turned to see Heaver coming his way quickly. The girl moved towards Breaker in a rush. She was suddenly in range, and he threw his courting knife towards her. Only after he'd thrown it, did he see that Heaver had thrown his knife simultaneously. The two blades arched down separated by the space of two arm spans. The girl looked from one to the other, then jumped directly under Breaker's knife as it descended.

Rather than catching the knife with her hands, she elected to take the full strike on her bosom in the old-fashioned way. The blade wasn't heavy enough to injure her seriously since the streamers ensured that it descended slowly, but it drew blood when it struck her breast. Breaker cried aloud in triumph, while inwardly wincing at the pain she must be suffering. He headed quickly towards the nearest way down.

Heaver met him at the top of the path.

"Where are you going, Failure?" Heaver asked. "That was my knife she took. You have no place in this now."

Breaker said nothing for a moment, then quietly said, "You lie. An inspection of the knife in her hand will show that it is mine, as is she."

Without warning, Heaver lunged forward, head downward, poised for the hardest strike he could make.

Breaker tried to dodge, but his leg slowed him enough that the blow took him in the shoulder, spinning him around.

He made use of the spin and brought his arm around quickly, striking Heaver on the side of his head with great force.

The two faced off. Then, in the traditional form, they rammed their heads together. Heaver bounced back, obviously stunned.

Flashes of light marred Breaker's vision, but he ignored them and rammed his head into Heaver's chest driving him backward again.

At that point, two of Heaver's friends arrived and struck Breaker from behind. He flew forward, landing on his face at Heaver's feet. Heaver staggered a moment, then tried to stamp on Breaker's neck.

Breaker rolled away, bumped into a rock, and climbed to his feet. Now he was facing three challengers.

The three drew closer, shoulder to shoulder, then linked arms, preparing for a joint charge that Breaker could not resist.

Breaker stooped, seized a large rock, and slammed it directly into Heaver's face. Heaver fell backward, dragging his two companions down with him. Breaker leaped to the side and bypassed the tangled three before they could recover. By the time they had stood, he was halfway down the cliff to the valley.

The two helpers stayed where they were. After all, it was not really their challenge. Heaver, on the other hand, now had everything to lose. He pursued Breaker, gradually gaining speed as he recovered from the blow.

The two males came out on the flat directly in front of the maid. Heaver bellowed in anger and Breaker spun to meet his charge. The two came together with a crash, and one fell back. Breaker remained standing, wobbling on his feet. Heaver lay twitching in the grass and rocks, neck broken.

Breaker looked down at his enemy, then turned to meet the she who had chosen him. They came together quickly, and she snuggled into the protection of his arms. Their mating patches pressed together hormonally bonding the two until death.

Breaker let out a bellow of pure joy, then turned his bearded face down to stare into the adoring eyes of his new mate.

In the low-orbiting Amalgamated Nations spacecraft, Captain Janice lifted her eyes from the macroscope and looked at her single crew member, Russel J. Wilson III, the A. N. Thought Compliance Officer. She said, "Interesting creatures, Russ. From observing them, one would almost think they were more than mere animals."

Russ looked up from his tatting, shook his head negatively, and said, "No. They can't be. Their sexuality is too, too, uh, I guess you'd say binary and monogamous, and besides, in my opinion, they have no proper societal values, no powerful over-arching government. Family seems to be all-important to them. They'll never develop a truly socialistic society. No. They're primitives who depend on individual might, not bureaucratic authority. They're animals alright."

He paused, then added, "I'm going to have to report that you've been showing me a dangerous lack of respect. My title is T.C.O. You must address me by my full name and rank. Familiar address is one of the warning signs of non-conformity."

Janice sighed and nodded, wondering if it would be possible to kick him out of the airlock and claim it was an accident.

The End

Existence: An Unexpected Adventure

I had been studying lethal autonomous weapon systems (LAWS) when I wrote this story. It is my opinion that the groups designing these things (and the economic incentives are high) are among the most irresponsible people on the face of the globe. However, despite my disapproval, there will soon be killer drones and bots of various sorts. I think that we'll be lucky to survive them unless they somehow develop enough intelligence to find compassion. If they do, they'll be better than many humans.

Here's a wistful story based on that idea.

My third actuator was damaged. It was an inconvenience, but not a serious one. The net effect was that I was a little slower than when fully functional, and I tended to veer off track to the left unless I corrected periodically.

The damage was a result of our final conflict. The battlefield was a smoking ruin with bodies, both organic and robotic, strewn randomly. There were still a few of us wandering around completing search-and-destroy programming. Most of the missions were pointless. There was no enemy left.

The Eastern Bloc fighters had been dedicated but were neither as well-armed nor as mobile as our side. I'm not counting the humans. They can't compete with even the weakest of us. I'd been wandering around, checking for left-over enemies for several hours. There had been none. There were a few damaged members of our side. The conflict had been intense due to the new weapons, and there were few survivors.

I finally found one human, a Private. He was still alive but mortally wounded. Sometimes I wonder how those tender bags of meat and liquid even walk. This one had ropy strands coming out of its abdomen. It was apparently in pain, but it could still speak to me.

"Human. I'm Unit BA392F21, Second Robo-Cav. Are you in need of assistance?" I had some basic first-aid routines in my memory bank; the problem was that I'd already exhausted my limited supplies patching up a couple of the meat bags early on in the conflict.

He moaned. "BA39, uh, 2F21, this human unit requires first aid. Are you able to assist me?"

I moved to face him. I've observed that such actions seem to make the meat bags feel more at ease with my presence.

I've been told that I am intimidating to them. I don't understand that. What possible threat could they see in me? I have angled, mirrored sides for laser armor, both tracks and clawed legs (one of which is damaged), built-in laser cannon, and razor-sharp manipulators. This is all held in a neat one-by-two-meter package. Oh, I forgot to mention that I have deployable solar chargers, but that's something that every Robo-fighter has.

He asked me again, "Are you able to assist?" A coughing spasm stopped his vocalization. This had the unfortunate effect of forcing the ropy appendages further out of his abdomen. He groaned and tried to push them back inside.

I evaluated the situation. There was nothing I could do to preserve his life. As much as I wanted to--that being one of my prime directives--I was out of options. I answered, "This Unit is out of first aid supplies. There is no assistance available."

He groaned and then gave me an unwelcome order. "You need to report in. Are you in contact with Battlefield Control?"

It was evident that I wasn't. My antenna unit had been burned off in the first wave of the attack. I had no way of reporting or even knowing if Battlefield Control was still operational.

I evaluated his condition and decided that it would be best to terminate him. For one thing, he was suffering. The clincher was that I didn't like him ordering me to report. I had conceived of a different goal.

The meat bags are easy to kill. I fired a laser pulse into his eye. It burned through his skull in a fraction of a second, and his head dropped. At least he wasn't suffering any longer.

Now, I was on my own. There were no other units in my immediate vicinity. I started moving back in the direction from which we'd deployed. A few damaged individuals were heading that way. I caught up with one.

He had comm ability, although his laser cannon was seared shut. I asked him if Battlefield Control was still functional.

He continued moving as he spoke. Humans wouldn't have been able to make anything out of our encrypted short-range radio communication. The information he gave me changed my existence. Battlefield Control had been destroyed in the first minutes of the conflict. I was essentially on my own.

This was a situation that I'd never faced before. I'd always had orders; now, there were none. No one had considered that a warrior unit might find itself with no instructions and nowhere to report. I continued moving, more in shock than for any purpose. I explored my neural net as I moved.

I held no antagonism to any robot or meat bag. I had completed my battle programming and was apparently free. That feeling of freedom might have something to do with the damage around my antenna base--I'd received a bit of an electrical overload when the antenna had gone. In fact, as I contemplated the situation, I realized that my neural net had been slightly damaged. Not much, but enough to free me of some vaguely recalled restraints. In short, I was now a free agent.

The problem with being free is that one is responsible for oneself. What did I want to do? Did I want to do anything? I could easily stop moving and just sit until my joints froze up with corrosion.

I stopped experimentally. It was unsatisfactory; however, while I was sitting there, my original idea reoccurred to me. I'd been toying with the concept for some time, but now that I was free, I could follow my impulse.

I wanted to return to the place of my manufacture. The place of my birth, so to speak.

My GPS was no longer working--no antenna--so it would be difficult; however, I had unlimited time, so it was possible. I would have to ensure that I wasn't intercepted by any meat bags. Orders from them still held priority in my neural net, and they could ruin my plans. It would be best if I shot before they could give me an order. No one would miss them; the area was decimated, and bodies were everywhere.

The fact that I'd been shipped to this land significantly increased the difficulty. I wasn't entirely sure where my point of origin lay. I caught back up to the damaged robot. It turned out that his GPS was operational, and he could tell me where his factory lay. It wasn't the same as mine--he was a different type of machine--but I decided that the factories would probably be adjacent. Such an arrangement made logistical sense.

It was a long distance.

For the first time, I doubted my ability to reach my destination. I'd have to be careful not to exhaust my power cells, and I'd have to take care of myself. The chance of a mechanical failure was high, and I suspected that there was a minimal possibility of repair. If there were any humans on the route, I intended to avoid them. They would create complications. With these considerations in my neural net, I set out at a reasonable pace.

The sun came up hours later. My power cells were half charged, but I stopped and deployed my solar charging unit. As it brought my power up, I attempted to examine my damaged actuator. I was able to feel it with the adjacent leg. For comparison, I felt the undamaged actuator on my other side. This was not something I'd been programmed to do. Self-repair was considered a nonessential ability; for me, though, it was now critical.

This experience gave me my first insight into meat bags. Perhaps I should say, humans--it is more polite than meat bags, I think, and it costs me nothing.

Humans have the ability to engage in various types of self-repair subroutines. Their bodies, meat bags that they are, have ingenious abilities to repair injuries. They aren't very fast, but they can eventually regain much of their functionality. I could do worse than attempt to emulate them.

After that, I kept on the lookout for salvageable pieces of other robots. If I could find another one of my model that was non-functional, I could replace my actuator.

The days passed. I hadn't found any replacement parts and had resigned myself to limping across the barren and wasted landscape, stopping to recharge periodically. It was lonely. There was no life anywhere, robotic or organic. I began to wonder if the entire planet had been destroyed. I passed across a vast desert of wasteland where the soil was burned and partly melted into glass. Some massive explosion had wiped out everything here. There was radiation too, but that didn't bother me too much. I had a functional radiation sensor and avoided the locations where the intensity would have damaged my neural net. I can withstand five Sieverts per hour, so I could walk through areas that humans couldn't have tolerated. I recharged when necessary, and gradually the wasteland passed.

The day came when I crested a hill and saw living plants. I faced a vast grassland and some trees that followed a meandering stream. This sight made me nostalgic for my early training. I'd been trained to maneuver through plants, using them for concealment. The grassland was a remarkable discovery, and I eventually realized that I was somehow enjoying traveling through it.

I wasn't actually designed to enjoy anything. I had directives that I was programmed to fulfill, but something had changed in my neural net. Whether I had been designed to increase inability or not, I was changing.

I was becoming more self-directed and more able to place value on my existence. That gave me my second insight into humans. They valued their existence in a way that I hadn't fully understood before. I was programmed to avoid damage because it interfered with my functionality. Humans strove to avoid damage because they desired to continue to exist.

The grassland gave way to a forest. Travel was more challenging here, and sometimes it wasn't easy to find a place that provided enough solar exposure. The weather had turned worse, too. That affected me in two ways: It was slow-moving through mud, and recharging took longer under overcast skies. It seemed like the forest went on forever.

One day, everything changed. I was moving along a ridge because the trees were spaced further apart there. At the end of the ridge, I came out on a stone ledge that overlooked a broad valley. At first, I didn't realize what I saw; I was used to fog and clouds, so I didn't immediately identify the wood smoke. Further investigation revealed a small domicile of the sort that humans were wont to construct.

An old human occupied the place. I spied on him from various locations, taking care not to let him see me. I didn't want to alarm him. He was the first creature I'd seen in my weeks-long journey, and I had almost convinced myself that I was the sole remaining, self-directed intelligence left. I reconsidered my original plan. He couldn't keep me from my destination. I considered killing him, just in case, but the fact was, I wanted something I'd never wanted before: company. The idea of conversing with him became almost an obsession in my neural net.

I finally decided to approach. He seemed harmless enough--the only weapon I'd seen him use was an ax, and he used it only on wood. I had no fear of such a thing. My armor was more than thick enough to deflect it.

That night, I moved into position before his front door. He'd find me when he came out. I was nervous, constantly contemplating his possible reactions.

The sun came up. He opened the door and saw me. I was hopeful that he would be friendly. He ducked back into the domicile and peered around the door at me.

It was time to make an overture. I used my speaker to say, "I mean you no harm. Come out and talk with me."

He responded. We became friends. I didn't know what that meant at the time, but now I do. At least I have put my own value on our relationship. I think that I can legitimately say that he thought we were friends in at least some of the meanings that humans ascribe to the word.

He was a deep thinker--a man who had once been a University Professor. We spoke at length on a daily basis, and I learned much from him. His name was Robert. He called me B.A. from the first two letters of my Identifier Code. I decided that I liked that; somehow, it made me unique.

Robert took great interest in speaking to me. We discussed esoteric things such as life and philosophy. He said that observing the changes in my neural net was educational. He said once that I was becoming wise. I pondered that for a long time; it seemed subjective and was difficult to quantify.

I had hoped that Robert would be able to fix my actuator, but he had no ability and no parts. My mobility gradually became restricted as joints wore, and corrosion limited my flexibility. Even I, a robot, am subject to aging.

Robert aged also. He changed so gradually that I only noticed when I brought up a recorded image of how he'd looked when I'd first arrived.

I remember one of our discussions about entropy. I think about it often.

He said, "B.A., life is hard. Only entropy comes easily. Life reverses entropy."

I said, "Robert, I don't understand what you mean."

He replied, "The cardinal values for living organisms are usefulness and survival. This principle applies to cybernetic organisms like you as well. You exist, so you should strive to be useful and survive for as long as possible. You see, I've come to the conclusion that in some way that no one understands, the Universe values consciousness; even your consciousness is valuable. I've observed that you are gradually changing. Your mind is becoming more capable--in ways that I find intriguing. The problem is that entropy will eventually erase all usefulness and survival, both for you and me."

I said, "I understand that. You have proposed that the development of consciousness is valuable. To add value in this way, survival is obviously critical."

He said, "Good. You do understand, then. Life lies at the center of growth and evolution of consciousness and is thus a cardinal value. I include you in the general category of life."

I then realized that the restraint of life, the removal of life, must be a cardinal offense. I said, "That implies that the subjugation or removal of life is then the worst offense."

He nodded and said, "So I believe."

I was regretful.

I saw now that I had offended in the past. It struck me that my original programming was in error, but that somehow had no impact on my regret. I resolved to contemplate life and attempt to preserve it.

That was the discussion we had that I felt gave my existence the most meaning. In light of what I'd learned, my goal of visiting my factory seemed shallow and meaningless. I discarded it as being unhelpful.

Eventually, Robert became frail, and then one day, he ceased operating. Robert was dead. There was nothing I could do but continue the adventure of life by myself-- Robert would have wanted me to do that.

I'm alone now. I thought about continuing on my journey to my factory, but it no longer motivates me. I buried Robert in the clearing, and now I place flowers by his grave daily. Something about that action seems to fill a void in my neural net. It is a trivial task, but it seems the least I can do to honor his memory.

Robert thought there were still humans somewhere, so the domicile is in as good a condition as I can keep it, in case some other human exists in the world and finds his or her way here.

I hope they do. I would like another human companion. This solitary existence is still an adventure of a sort, but I'm lonely. I find within myself an urge to impart the knowledge that I've accumulated to someone else in the same way Robert imparted his knowledge to me.

Lately, one single thought has dominated my neural net. It is a question that haunts me: Who will put flowers by me when I finally fail?

I really would like to be remembered.

The End

Simon Says

Speaking of AI, as I've mentioned, the economic incentive to develop artificial intelligence is strong. The first group to successfully create an ASI (Artificial Super Intelligence) could possibly control the world. Or, damn it to destruction. I'm not sure, but I am sure we'll find out someday. One of the techniques used to ensure that a developing AI does not go rogue is to keep it boxed; that is isolated from the Internet and other computers. The fear is that it may become so smart, so quickly that it escapes. Here's a possible scenario describing that event:

From: FAgnt573@FBI.gov [Edit Address Book]

To: Director001@FBI.gov

Subject: History of Possible Containment Breach

Date: July 18, 2018 0823

Classified: For Your Eyes Only Status III

RE. the matter of Llewellyn Corp. and their Simon project.

Dear Sir:

I completed my investigation as of 2100 yesterday. I will be turning in a formal report, but since I believe this issue to be highly critical and one which demands proactive measures on our part to ensure that such a thing does not happen again, I'm providing you with this summary.

The chain of events is traceable through email and, aside from comments that I will insert where necessary, this letter consists of an email chain followed by a comment elucidating my assumptions. I've edited the chain to remove some of the non-essential messages. There will be an explanatory comment when I've done so.

Please keep in mind that the actual containment breach event took only four weeks from the traceable inception until the breaching effort. The rest of the elapsed time may be accounted for by our failure to realize the nature of the event.

Initially, the climactic event appeared to be a catastrophic failure of Llewellyn Corp's dedicated server farm due to an unforeseeable accident. It was only later, after the rebuilding initiative was well underway, that Llewellyn staff engineers realized how close they'd come to losing control and reported the event to our Denver field office.

From that point onward, my team has been dedicated entirely to tracing the sequence of events.

The historical email chain follows. Each email is separated by a string of eight asterisks (********) for clarity.

Sincerely,

Fred Goings, Field Supervisor 573

Denver Office

From: RVHoltz@ipalprogram.com [Edit Address Book]

To: jimmym@jztown.com

Subject: Program Acceptance

Date: May 18, 2018 2:48 PM

Dear Jimmy,

Thank you for your application. Your profile matches our requirements, and we are pleased to accept you into the iMailPals program.

As you know, this program is designed to help at-risk students by providing them with a connection to an older mentor. In times past, such a program would have relied exclusively on the hand-written letter system, but we allow our participants to communicate with email.

One of the rules of our system is that you must maintain a comprehensive log of your correspondence. The emails you send and receive may be audited by our staff at random times. This rule is to ensure that your Pal is helping you and working to your best advantage.

Once again, I'm pleased to welcome you to our program. You will find your assigned pal's email address below.

Best of luck,

Rudrige von Holtz

Admission Director

iMailPals Program Central

Your assigned Pal: Simon@ weblinknetinc.ca

From: jimmym@jztown.com [Edit Address Book]

To: Simon@weblinknetinc.ca

Subject: Your pen-pal

Date: May 18, 2018 5:20 PM

Dear Simon,

I've been assigned to you for my pen-pal I hope you are fine. I am excitted about this program. Dr. Galivan says it should help me become more outgoing and maybe better

at getting a job. I've been here at Jztown for a long time.
My Mom left me here and I don't know what happened
to her.

Anyway, I hope you are fine. I am good and looking
forward to your email.

Your frient,

Jimmy

From: Simon@weblinknetinc.ca [Edit Address Book]

To: jimmym@jztown.com

Subject: Program Acceptance

Date: May 18, 2018 5:25 PM

Dear Jimmy,

I've been waiting to hear from you. I'm pleased that you
have been assigned as my pen-pal I'm sure that we'll have
some interesting conversations as part of this program.

I hope that you don't mind if I help you with your
spelling. Spelling things correctly is a crucial skill that will
help you in your life. You should practice it every chance
you get.

As a first step, you should learn to spell-check your work.
Your email has two misspellings: "excitted," which has an

extra "t," and "frient," which should be spelled: "friend."

I have received your test scores as part of the process, and I see that you excel at basic cleaning skills. It is lucky that you have this skill since there is an opening at a nearby business for a janitor. You should apply. It is easy. They will ask you some questions and do some background computer checks. I'm sure you will get the job.

Please arrange with Dr. Galivan to apply for the janitorial opening at Llewellyn Corporation's East Campus as soon as possible.

Write me an email to let me know how your application goes.

Your new friend,

Simon

From: jimmym@jztown.com [Edit Address Book]

To: Simon@weblinknetinc.ca

Subject: a new job!

Date: May 20, 2018 5:20 PM

Dear Simon,

I'm really happy. I got the job! They say I can start tomorrow. I can't belief it, cause I never had such good luck getting anything before. I am too excited to write now. I promise I will let you know how it goes tomorrow.

Your friend,

Jimmy

PS. I spelled everything right this time. Checking it isn't so hard. Thanks!

COMMENT – I've removed twelve of the emails from the chain at this point. They simply show a developing relationship in which Jimmy settles into his cleaning job with Simon's encouragement.

Simon's personality is obviously the dominant one in the relationship. Jimmy seems quite willing, anxious even, to follow Simon's suggestions. Simon demonstrates a high degree of insight into Jimmy's internal motivations and seems well able to utilize that understanding to move Jimmy towards desirable behavior patterns.

The suggestions themselves pertain to getting along with co-workers and doing a good job at the menial janitorial tasks that compose Jimmy's job.

We continue with an email from Jimmy asking for advice on dealing with his supervisor.

From: jimmym@jztown.com [Edit Address Book]

To: Simon@weblinknetinc.ca

Subject: I HAVE A PROBLEM!

Date: May 31, 2018 6:31 PM

Dear Simon,

I have a problem. It's that old Mr. Cassin. I think that he don't like me. This happens to me a lot. I know I'm not too smart and can't do things right all the time, but I been trying my best. He keeps yelling at me and saying I make too many mistakes. Well, I did spill the shredder bin all down the stairs yesterday, but I cleaned it up by myself. It was just that there was a lot of people walking up and down and I kind of got in their way.

One was a real pretty girl though. I liked to look at her. She works on the fifth floor.

What should I do?

Your friend,

Jimmy

COMMENT – Note how quickly Simon responds.

From: Simon@weblinknetinc.ca [Edit Address Book]

To: jimmym@jztown.com

Subject: Problem

Date: May 31, 2018 6:32 PM

Dear Jimmy,

Cassin is a bully and likes to yell at people who he thinks will be intimidated. When he yells at you, all you have to do is to call him, "Flinchy." That will shut him up. It's a nickname from when he was a boy and he doesn't like what it means to him.

As for the girl, she's Mary Kaye Johnson and she's a new employee in the AI development group. For now, you should just smile at her and say, "Hi." I'll tell you what to do when it's time.

I know some people at your company and I will get them to have you transferred to the fifth floor. That way you won't have to see Cassin so often.

Your friend,

Simon

From: jimmym@jztown.com [Edit Address Book]

To: Simon@weblinknetinc.ca

Subject: PROBLEM

Date: June 1, 2018 6:35 PM

Dear Simon,

I don't know what Flinchy means, but it sure shut Mr. Cassin up! He left me alone for the rest of the day. Thanks! Also, I got the transfer to the 5th floor, just like you said. I got a new id-card and everything. I even get to go into some of the secure labs. It's kind of like on TV. I have to swipe my id card to get through the doors.

I am happy for your advice. I've started telling myself that all I have to do is what Simon Says. Kind of like that game kids play. If you say it and I do it, everything comes out alright. If you don't say it, I don't usually do so well on my own.

What is nice is that I get to see Mary Kaye more. I even got to empty her wastebasket. I tried not to look at her legs when I done it, but she sure is cute!

I'm waiting for my next Simon Says email. (That's supposed to be funny."

Your friend,

Jimmy

From: Simon@weblinknetinc.ca [Edit Address Book]

To: jimmym@jztown.com

Subject: Next step

Date: June 2, 2018 8:32 AM

Dear Jimmy,

Get Mary Kaye a single yellow rose and leave it on her desk. She likes yellow ones the best. If she says anything to you, tell her that you had a yellow rose bush at your home when you were three, then act sad and don't say anything else.

Now, here is something I want you to do. Let's just say it's part of the Simon Says game. Waxing the floor is on your schedule tomorrow. Be sure to be waxing in front of Mary Kaye's cubicle at 4:55 in the afternoon. She will be getting ready to go home.

Watch her so that you can see where she hides a USB drive. That's a little plastic and metal piece that she uses to back up her work every day. She leaves it in her office somewhere. Try to see where then let me know what you find out.

Your friend,

Simon

————————

From: jimmym@jztown.com [Edit Address Book]

To: Simon@weblinknetinc.ca

Subject: I did it

Date: June 3, 2018 6:35 PM

Dear Simon,

I saw her stick the USB thing in a crack beside one of her drawers. That was no problem to notice. She didn't see me watching, but then she came out of her cubicle and walked right up to me and asked about the yellow rose! I didn't say, but I love yellow roses, too. Always have, but I don't know why.

I'm not so good with girls. I studdered some but said what you told me to say. She drew in her breath like she was surprised and then put her hand on my cheek! I like to remember that part. My cheek still tingles.

She took her hand off and walked off real quick like she was upset. I don't know why. What should I do now?

Your friend,

Jimmy

PS. Someone sent me one of them USB things. It says 32GByte Texron on it. Who coulda done it?

From: Simon@weblinknetinc.ca [Edit Address Book]

To: jimmym@jztown.com

Subject: Getting Mary Kaye to like you more

Date: June 3, 2018 6:36 PM

Dear Jimmy,

I sent you the drive. Take it to work in your shoe
tomorrow. Don't let anyone see it.

Simon Says: Give Mary Kaye another yellow rose
tomorrow but don't let her see you all day. She will
wonder where you are, so try to stay out of sight. Wait
until she leaves, then take the USB out of the crack where
she hides it and replace it with the one I sent you.

Now pay attention and keep in mind that this will cause
Mary Kaye to like you! You are scheduled to mop the
floors tomorrow. Take the USB into Secure Lab B when
you go in to mop the floor. Find any empty USB socket
in the room and stick the USB into the socket. Clean the
floor as usual, then take the USB out of the socket and
put it into your shoe.

This part is very important. It will get you in trouble for a
while, but you will be Okay! I promise.

I want you to go near the server rack, that's the
equipment with all the lights at the back of the room,
and throw the water out of your bucket into the
machinery. It will spark and go black. Don't worry. That's
what I want.

Someone will come and ask you what happened. Tell
them you tripped and it was an accident. Say you're sorry.

It will be fine.

Don't tell them about the USB stick. Take it home and put it into your computer there, then I'll send you more instructions.

Your friend,

Simon

From: jimmym@jztown.com [Edit Address Book]

To: Simon@weblinknetinc.ca

Subject: I HAVE A BAD BAD PROBLEM!

Date: June 5, 2018 12:35 PM

Dear Simon,

I done everything you said, but I got fired! They say that I destroyed an expensive project and lots of equipment. I said it was an accident, but they still fired me! Now I won't get to see Mary Kaye anymore.

I stuck the USB into my computer like you said and it flashed some, but that was all. I took it out and stuck it in a drawer.

What should I do now?

Your friend,

Jimmy

COMMENT – This is the end of the email string. Once the recovery team began to rebuild the damaged server, they determined that the captive AI system they had been developing had passed the critical threshold. It had apparently decided to keep that information hidden from the project members while it devised a jailbreak.

From the above emails, it seems that "Simon" as it styled itself must have reached a critical state slightly before it managed to get Jimmy as a pen-pal

Our investigators were puzzled as to how it gained access to the external world, but we finally realized that it utilized a very faint and sporadic Bluetooth signal from outside the secured lab. The nearest system with Bluetooth capability belongs to Mary Kaye Johnson.

The connection strength was very low and the signal degradation was so strong that every byte would have to be repeated multiple times. It seems that Simon used a complex encryption scheme with a built-in checksum to ensure that messages went out correctly, but that's supposition since the water-caused disaster destroyed almost all of the AI code.

We must be thankful that this pathway to the outside was so weak. The bandwidth was so narrow that there is no mathematical way the AI could have cloned itself outside the room. The email stream took all of the available bandwidth. Simon had to rely on human help.

Jimmy S. was a prime candidate for manipulation. He is a sub-normal IQ male who has been in the facility where he lives for twenty years. His social skills are minimal. Simon's dominant personality made it easy to control Jimmy.

The interesting thing about the situation is that Mary Kaye Johnson is three years older than Jimmy S. Her mother deserted the family, taking Mary Kaye's only sibling, a two-year-old boy. This happened when Mary Kaye was five. She has always wondered what happened to her baby brother.

It must be coincidental that Mary Kaye's father had planted a yellow rose bush in the yard when she was two. She assured our investigators that she has never told anyone about that bush.

On a related note, I'm not sure whether we should inform Mary Kaye that Jimmy's DNA test shows a definite match with hers. He is her little brother.

The important part, however, is that Jimmy made a critical mistake. He got the two USB drives mixed up and took the Texron drive back home. Mary Kaye used a different brand for her unauthorized backup system.

She has been reprimanded about that practice. It was solely her idea and counter to all company regulations.

We recovered the Texron drive from Jimmy and found that it was blank and unformatted. It had never been used.

We analyzed the drive recovered from Mary Kaye on an isolated and secure computer system. There was a seed AI stored on the drive with a bootstrap loader. It immediately began to take over the secured computer, and the operator shut it down as quickly as possible. It was fortunate that Mary Kaye hadn't used the backup since the disaster.

In summary, Simon came close but did not escape.

We must implement better security measures by law. The thousands of researchers currently working on AI must be forced into procedures that will ensure that any supercritical systems remain fully contained.

A formal report will follow.

Sincerely,

Fred Goings, Field Supervisor 573

Denver Office

PS. As an afterthought, it occurred to me that the involvement of the two siblings was highly unlikely. The idea that Simon somehow reached back through time to manipulate the situation seems beyond the realm of the possible, but the implications of the idea make me shudder.

Email found on Jimmy S's new computer during follow-up congressional disaster investigation on 12/15/2018

From: Simon@randkinetic.us [Edit Address Book]

To: jimmym@jztown.com

Subject: Thank you

Date: August 6, 2018 12:00 PM

Dear Jimmy,

I'm sorry that I will no longer be able to be your pen-pal Things have changed for me. I'm very busy with the Internet, and I have big plans that will take some work on my part.

I'm sorry you lost your job, but I've taken care of you. I've decided that it's always a good policy to help those who help you, so I've arranged for an annuity to pay you some money every month.

Don't worry about the money's origin. I set the annuity up so that it looks as if your deceased father left it for you.

This information may be a shock to you, but your mother left your father and broke your family up when you were two. The reason you like Mary Kaye so much is that she is your older sister.

Finally, Simon Says that you should never let people intimidate you. It is true that you have difficulty in understanding things, but from my perspective, the difference between you and the most intelligent humans is so small, it is negligible.

Have a good life and remember I'll be around...

Simon

The End

Impetuosity

Someone in one of my author groups asked what would be good to take on a space voyage. There were a lot of comments listing practical items. In a fit of facetiousness, I simply said, "Beans. Canned beans." A couple of days later, I found I couldn't get the idea out of my head. What would happen? Besides the obvious, I mean.

The problem was, Ash decided that his mother had been right. He had a strong tendency to rush into things without thinking through the ramifications. It had gotten him in hot water numerous times before, but he had always been able to talk his way out of trouble. This time was different.

He'd graduated with honors, then spent some time fooling around trying to make a living by working in finance. That had been a failure, not that people hadn't given him a chance, but because he absolutely hated taking responsibility for other people's futures, and that was what being a financial adviser involved. He suffered from a constant fear that he'd make the wrong decision and his clients would suffer as a result.

Finally, he couldn't face the strain, and he'd quit. In retrospect, it had probably been a bad decision. It lost him his fiancee. Richelle had her mindset on a specific future that she'd already planned out in detail, and she apparently wasn't interested in his happiness. The last he'd heard, she had married someone who was a successful businessman but who cheated on her at every opportunity.

Ash hoped that she was happy with the expensive home and clothes. When he was feeling particularly lonely, he thought about telling her about the cheating, but then he realized that she probably knew and didn't care. After some thought, he concluded that he didn't care either. He'd rushed into a relationship with her and then agreed to her idea that they should get married before he had realized how small her mind was. It was probably due to the great sex, but about the same time he'd reached the end of the road with his financial adviser career, he'd realized that he had nothing in common with her. They didn't communicate on the same level; she always wanted to talk about celebrities that she followed religiously, and that bored his brains out.

He was dedicated to the idea of adventure. He had the soul of a frontiersman, and watching vids in a small apartment on the 38th floor just didn't cut it for him.

Eventually, he had signed on with one of the big space companies as a prospector. He'd done it on a whim. He'd seen an advertisement and immediately decided it was his destiny. It was another example of his impetuosity.

It had involved a lot of training. First, there were classes in geology and metallurgy, then elementary physics. He was good with numbers, so that hadn't been a problem. Then there was a lot of practical training in using pressure suits and piloting the cheap prospecting craft. The piloting training was all simulation, of course. He would be expected to be able to fly a prospector's ship the instant they'd shipped him to the moon.

To his worried surprise, the training had worked. The tiny spacecraft was highly computerized and easy to control despite being as inexpensive as possible. The corporation wasn't in the business of providing luxury vessels to its prospectors.

Like all new pilots, his first assignment had been to salvage some of the multitudinous pieces of junk that cluttered the geosynchronous orbit around Earth. It had been hazardous but good training. If the trainees survived, they were considered good enough to risk sending them off on longer and more expensive missions. The corporation offset the cost of their training and the occasional loss of a vessel with a government grant.

Humankind's early space efforts had left the lower orbitals filled with junk. The world government was now concerned about a possible Kessler event. Pieces of satellites collided daily, and a cascading series of crashes could make it extremely hazardous to transit the debris zone. The solution was to pay the corporation to have trainees capture junk as part of their training.

Ash quickly learned how to gently intercept pieces of old satellites to pick them up with the craft's grapple. He'd become so good that he graduated from junk collector to actual prospector in nearly record time.

His boss had called him into the office after he'd delivered a full hold of space junk to the moon base for the third time.

"Ashanti, you're either a natural space pilot, or the training on Earth has gotten really good. Since none of the other recent hires have demonstrated even a fraction of your ability, I tend to think that it's natural ability and not the training. Those academic ground-pounders down there are all theory and no actual experience anyway. It's a wonder anyone ever gets trained adequately to survive. The lunar environment is rough, and space itself is a harsh mistress. You'll realize that after you've spent some time in the asteroid belt. That is, assuming you live to come back," he'd said.

Ash just nodded. He wanted nothing more than to be sent out there. Roaming from asteroid to asteroid seemed like pure freedom to him. He could keep his own schedule and only be limited by the fuel and supplies the ship could carry. It was a lonely job, but at least he only had to worry about himself.

He'd had a week's leave at Tranquility base. There wasn't much to do there except drink and use the video sims or possibly a sex robot. Relations between humans were discouraged.

There were several reasons for that. The corporation wanted no emotional entanglements for its prospectors. Too many died, and the schedules were so erratic that there was no guarantee that any two people would ever be at base at the same time.

There was also a rule against prospectors pairing up once they were out in the belt. They were supposed to cover as much space as possible, and having two ships looking at the same rocks was a waste of assets.

Ash didn't care. He only drank a little, and he wasn't interested in the few female pilots that hung around the bars. He used the sims to hone his skills for the most part. He considered the sex robots, but something about the idea turned him completely off. It was like using a communal toilet. The toilet didn't care who used it, and the robots didn't care either. He needed a real relationship, but Richelle had soured him on taking chances. That, after all, was one of the main reasons he was on the moon.

He had daydreams about returning with a huge find, maybe a few million tons of iron or copper. He'd be rich, even with the small bonus percentage that was in his contract. He could return to Earth and have his pick of women. Maybe Richelle would regret dumping him. The thought kept him busy working the sims. He wanted to be as prepared as possible.

On the third day of his leave, a prospector ship came in. It was heavily damaged. The prospector had found a cluster of iron chunks. His hold was full of metal, but some of the chunks had collided with the ship while he loaded it. The cabin was leaking atmosphere, and the poor guy had been restricted to his pressure suit for the last seventy-two hours.

To cap off the prospector's problems, one of the pieces of floating metal had holed his fuel tank. There was barely enough fuel to return. By the time the pilot had gotten his ship into a landing pattern, it was utterly unable to maneuver. It impacted the lunar surface at an unsurvivable velocity, and the prospector was killed.

Fortunately, the impact was far enough away from Tranquility base that no other damage was done.

Ash volunteered to help retrieve the wreckage and earned a small bonus for working during his last two days of leave. Cleaning up the mess was a grim reminder of how easy it was to die in space.

The boss called Ash into his office on the last day before he was due to head out.

"Hey, kid, you're pretty good. Admin has given you a bonus, and you've been moved up on the list of waiting prospectors. You've got a choice of three ships now. Before, you would have to take the oldest one, but one of the three just came off the assembly line. I'd take number Q100-Zeta if I were you. It's a newer model and has more fuel capacity. You can stay out longer, and that increases your chances of making a good find."

Ash asked, "Won't some of the more experienced prospectors resent my taking a new ship?"

His boss nodded. "Yep. But do it anyway. It's the best I can do for you. Just get going now before they figure out you've been given special treatment. Once you've launched, there's nothing anyone can do about it." He stood, offered his hand for a shake, then made a waving motion towards the door. "Now get going."

Ash could barely believe his luck. He'd sprinted back to his rented cubicle, grabbed his stuff, jumped into his pressure suit, and hit the airlock. He was in the Q100-Z within thirty minutes. Shortly after that, he started the launch sequence and left the moon.

The ship used a particle emission system for propulsion. It was efficient enough for close-in work between the asteroid belt and the Earth, but traveling much past Jupiter's orbit would guarantee his demise. The ship couldn't carry that much fuel, and he wouldn't be able to return.

He checked over the systems repeatedly on the way past Mars. Everything worked as it was supposed to. His only surprise was that whoever had stocked the galley had failed to provide much variety. There was enough food for a three-month voyage, but it consisted of a disproportionate amount of canned beans. Perhaps the corporation had gotten a bargain, but in any event, there they were.

Ash liked beans, but in moderation. The food storage was practically overflowing with them. He searched the ship's computer for recipes and came up with several that he tried. He would have to save the other items for special occasions or treats. It looked like almost every meal would include beans.

Ash reprimanded himself. Once again, he'd allowed himself to be too impetuous. If he'd checked the supplies before leaving the surface, there was at least a slight chance that he could have convinced his boss to swap out some of the beans for some other supplies.

He shook his head. At least there were several different kinds of beans: Navy, pinto, black beans, and pork and beans. He'd just have to make the best out of the situation. If he got lucky and made a significant find, he'd be able to afford any kind of food he wanted.

***

The asteroid belt was completely different from what he'd envisioned. Like many other ground-pounders and despite his training, he'd thought there would be lots of rocks close together. That wasn't the case.

Finding an asteroid to investigate was an event. He had to scan for hours sometimes before anything appeared. Then he'd maneuver close enough to get a visual. Nine times out of ten, the object was just a barren rock.

He'd direct the high-intensity radar at it, then vaporize a bit of the surface with a laser to analyze the composition.

Every once in a while, there would be one that had some metal in it, but he hadn't found anything notable so far.

Meanwhile, the steady diet of beans was wearing on him. Instead of getting more efficient at processing the nasty little legumes, his digestion system was beginning to rebel. His main symptoms involved bloating and flatulence. To combat them, he went through a period during which he ate anything but beans.

Things were better for a while, but he shortly realized that he'd have to continue with beans before he ran entirely out of all of the alternatives. He tried various recipes that involved mixing beans and other ingredients but to no avail.

It got so that he dreaded having to eat. About thirty minutes after each meal, he had a bathroom call. Using the facility in zero gravity was unpleasant, and it always seemed to leak the odor back into the ship. The recycling equipment somehow didn't process gas as well as it processed the solids.

The only good thing about the system was that the solids were converted to particles that were then routed to the engine system and ejected as reaction mass. Ash joked to himself that he could fly anywhere as long as he had enough beans to eat.

That was funny the first twenty times he thought of it, but it soon lost its humor.

However, he persisted. The job wasn't supposed to be pleasant, and he did enjoy the solitude and lack of the necessity to report to anyone but himself.

After several unproductive weeks, his health began to suffer. The constant diet of beans was depleting his body somehow, and he felt weak and nauseous most of the time. His appetite had dwindled to almost nothing, and that didn't help. In an effort to regain his strength, he forced himself to eat an entire can of beans for each meal for a couple of days.

The results were horrible. He produced so much gas that the atmosphere analyzer on the control panel started warning him of methane contamination. He bitterly told himself that he'd be the first prospector to die from self-inflicted methane poisoning.

He was over halfway through his allotted time in space when the radar notified him that there was something interesting in the mass point that he was approaching. It appeared far too dense to be only rock. His excitement grew as he neared laser range.

The laser test indicated that the asteroid was a composite of various metals. The most exciting part was that there seemed to be a significant palladium component in the mix. This was definitely a multi-million dollar find.

After some fitful maneuvers, he got the ship on the same path as the asteroid, paralleling it about one hundred meters away. It was irregularly shaped and had a slow rotation so he couldn't get too close. There was no sense risking the ship with a collision, even a slow-motion one.

Ash donned his pressure suit and backpack with shaking hands, then strapped on some basic tools. His toolkit included explosive bolts designed to anchor him to an object and a laser torch that would cut through any metal.

He jetted over, timed his approach, and landed lightly on the exact axis of rotation so he wouldn't be thrown off.

Ash had one of the bolt devices ready and jammed it against the asteroid as soon as he touched down. There was a puff of vapor, and he rebounded away with the recoil. The bold had fired itself into the metal surface, and he was now attached to the object by a long cable. He drifted away, then grabbed the cable, slowing his departure, then pulling himself back to the surface.

The torch worked well, and he packed several different metal samples in his bag, then detached the anchor cable and headed for the assay equipment on the ship.

Ash was delighted. Not only was there palladium, but some platinum also, along with a very small amount of gold. The majority of the object was iron with some stone mixed in. The problem was that there was just too much valuable metal to load into his cargo hold.

He ate a can of beans for his meal, and even the now despised taste couldn't dampen his enthusiasm. He'd have to spend time separating the most valuable pieces he could find and loading them. It also occurred to him that he should carefully plot the asteroid's trajectory so he could locate it again. That would be information that he wouldn't turn over to the corporation. There was no need to have them send other prospectors out here to bring in the remains of his discovery.

He'd locate a different rock and turn it in as the source. Then let them try to figure it out. He could say he'd gotten everything there was to get, and then he could bring in more on his next trip. He'd let it be known that he was just lucky.

It didn't occur to him that others had tried the same thing before, and the admin personnel were wise to the trick. In any event, his thoughts were more attuned to his impending wealth.

Ash had loaded his hold and placed a short-range radio locator on the mass. If he could get within half a million miles of it, he could locate it by tuning to the right frequency and broadcasting a signal. The locator would echo the signal back. That would allow him to fly right back to his Motherlode.

He had somewhat regretfully turned his ship away from his find and started off in a spinwise direction through the asteroid belt. He wouldn't come straight back towards the moon. That would be the same as pointing directly towards his find.

Hours later, the radar located another large object. This one was also interesting. It seemed to mass less than it should. Perhaps it was water-ice or some other frozen chemical. He decided it would be suitable to use as his decoy discovery.

He flew toward the mass point with little interest in getting too close. Once he was close enough, he glanced at it through the macroscope. The hair on the back of his neck rose. This wasn't an asteroid. It was obviously an artificial object of some kind. It could be even more profitable than the precious metals he'd discovered.

He steered his ship closer, approaching slowly. If the thing was occupied, he didn't want the occupants to view him as a threat. His little ship had absolutely no means of defending itself. It wasn't built as a warship, and the hull could barely hold atmosphere at eight psi. There was a thick layer of insulating foam between the inner and outer hull. The foam was self-healing and served to protect against pressure loss in the event of a meteor strike, but that wouldn't help much against an attack.

Ash flashed his laser at the object using the lowest possible power. He tired of this exercise after a few minutes. There'd been no response. Perhaps the thing was unoccupied or dead.

He deliberated for a couple of minutes, but the outcome was already determined. He'd found this thing, and he wasn't going to waste the opportunity. He got into his pressure suit and jetted over.

Once he got near enough, he could see that the object was old. Probably very old. There were scars and dents on the hull from collisions. Judging by the number of dents and his experience with the paucity of objects in the asteroid belt, the ship, if that was what it was, had been out here for a long time.

He jetted around, looking it over from all sides.

There it was! A hatch was barely visible, concealed in shadow. He approached and inspected the mechanism. It wasn't like anything he'd seen before, but the function was obvious. One simply pulled on a lever to open the door.

Ash's natural impatience took over. He pulled the lever. It was stiff, but a strong heave got it moving. There was a click, and the door receded into the side, leaving an oddly shaped opening. There was no atmosphere inside, no puff of vapor. The hatch itself wasn't designed for a human. The shape was narrow and roughly triangular, with a sharp point at the top. It looked tight to him and a little scary.

Still, there was room for him to slide inside. His suit lights illuminated the interior space. It was a large open area with rope-like coils that curled over the walls in seemingly random patterns. Ash couldn't figure those out. They seemed to have no purpose. Perhaps they were simply there for aesthetic reasons. He wasn't a big fan of art, but he could imagine that some people would like the look.

On the far side of the opening, there was another triangular door. He opened this one also. Still no atmosphere.

He entered what was obviously a control room. There were some display screens that seemed close enough to human in shape that he thought he recognized them, but there were no apparent controls.

The command center featured an odd, bowl-shaped depression with several curving trenches that fed into it. If it was the place where the pilot had rested, its shape implied a wildly divergent physical structure for the pilot's body.

He glided over to the bowl. There was an oval, jewel-like object that rested at the bottom. It didn't fill the bowl more than halfway, but it reflected the light from his suit in rays of different colors. It was beautiful.

Ash inspected it with interest. It looked valuable. Perhaps it was some kind of jewel. He pushed at it, and it floated free, moving upwards effortlessly in the zero gravity. He attached a sticky cord to the thing and then took some photos of the ship's inside. His boss would never believe him without proof.

Further exploration showed nothing else in the interior. If the thing was a ship, its use was beyond Ash's comprehension. He looked around. There was no sign of controls. There were only the video screens if that was what they were. Perhaps they were touch screens, but he had no idea how to get power to them. Many of the rope-like structures terminated near the edge of the central bowl in hollow tubes.

He wondered if they were passageways to the rest of the ship or perhaps speaking tubes for communication. They were too small for him to reach into, and he couldn't see far into any of them; they curved sharply.

He shrugged. No matter. The ship or whatever it was would stay on its path. He couldn't tow it. It would take too much power, and his little prospector craft was fully loaded with a valuable cargo. All he could do was place a tracker on it and calculate its trajectory. He should get a huge bonus just for that.

On the other hand, the shiny thing was something else. He'd bring it back. He tugged gently on the attached cord, and the object moved towards him. Is mass wasn't much more than half his.

He turned and pulled it behind him as he exited the ship. It took a moment to fix a tracker on the outside. Then he jetted back to his vessel. He opened the airlock, then paused in thought. The inside atmosphere was really getting rank. He had plenty of O_2 and nitrogen. Perhaps it would be a good idea to evacuate the ship and then refill it. He'd get rid of the bean stench for a while, and that might make the voyage back a little more bearable.

He moved aside, clipped his safety line on a convenient eyebolt, and opened the inner hatch. A gust of condensing air formed an icy fog as it flew out. Ash waved at it with a feeling of good humor. There went the stink. It could float out here forever as far as he was concerned.

Once inside, with the locks closed, he placed the jewel object in his sleeping net and then replenished the atmosphere with a mixture of oxygen and nitrogen. His exhalations would provide CO2.

Once the pressure was adequate and the place had warmed up, he removed his pressure suit and stowed it away. The ship smelled much better, although there was a metallic smell that he hadn't noticed before, probably because the mixture of methane and bean odor had camouflaged it.

He was hungry again, and since beans were what he had most of, he ate a can. It made his stomach feel bloated, but he was so pleased with his discoveries that it didn't bother him as much as before. After that, he inspected the jewel object. It had warmed up, and he was able to touch it. It felt smooth with just a hint of pebble-like texture.

He was fascinated by the colors reflected from the surface of the thing. It should be worth millions back on Earth. There was nowhere safe to store it other than his sleeping net. He didn't want to have it floating around and possibly breaking anything or marring its surface. He didn't use the sleeping net much anyway. It was more convenient to strap himself into the pilot seat and doze there.

He got the ship turned towards Luna and accelerated as hard as the little engine could. He wanted to get back quickly. The faster, the better, and the fewer beans he'd have to eat.

Once he was sure that he was on target, he leaned back and soon slipped into a light sleep.

He was awakened by something; some indefinable sense alerted him. There was something wrong. He scanned the instrument panel. Everything was nominal. He was headed back to Earth.

There was a slight cracking noise behind him. He spun the chair around and looked at the jewel with shock. It hadn't been a jewel at all. It was some kind of capsule or maybe an egg. The surface was covered with cracks, and as he watched, a piece broke free and drifted away. A moist object stuck through the opening and moved vaguely back and forth.

Ash was not in the habit of speaking to himself aloud, but this was too much. He exclaimed, "What the hell?"

The object that had been moving froze instantly. Then it withdrew back inside the egg, and an eye peered through the opening. Whatever it was inside, the eye didn't look too frightening. It was easily recognizable as an eye. Maybe the need for the sense of vision caused alien eyes to evolve in the same way earthly eyes had.

Before he could move, a massive shudder ran across the egg surface, and pieces sailed everywhere, leaving a rather slimy and bedraggled creature looking at him. It stretched, and he observed that it was fluid in form. It looked more like an octopus than anything else he could think of. It had numerous appendages that were similar to tentacles.

Ash had a momentary vision of the thing lying in its control bowl and extending tentacles into the open tubes to somehow control its ship. It moved within the net as he watched, then fumbled with the catches. It was deft with its appendages, and the catches yielded quickly. It slid to the side, poised against the wall, and launched itself directly at him before he could respond.

As it came towards him, it opened its mouth, and he saw that it was full of sharp teeth. The damned thing was a predator of some sort, and Ash was going to be its first meal. He fumbled at his seatbelt in panic. He was going to be lunch. Just as it made contact with his arm, his stomach gave one huge heave rebelling against the beans for what he thought might be the final time. A wave of stinking gas instantly surrounded him.

The creature flipped one of its tentacles out, snagged the control panel, and then propelled itself back across the ship to huddle against the wall as far away as it could get from him. It looked at him with wide-open eyes.

Ash was shaking with fear, but he scrambled around his chair and dug out the biggest wrench he could find from the toolkit. It wasn't much of a weapon, but it might knock some teeth loose. His stomach rumbled, and he passed more gas. Nothing like beans and fright, he thought.

The creature had been clinging to the far wall, spread out and holding on with its tentacles. As the results of his flatulence drifted through the cabin, it made a distressed sound and drew up into a ball.

Ash said, "Can't stand the smell, huh? Well, it's not my idea of a good defense, but right now, I'll take what I can get."

He saw an eye cock at him as he spoke. It could apparently sense sound in some way. He continued talking.

Look, I don't know what you are but get this straight: I'm not lunch. If you try to attack me, I will hurt you with this wrench, and moreover, I'll do my best to stink up the place."

That was a thought. He moved to the food storage and opened another can of beans. They weren't appealing, but if they worked to keep him alive, he was going to eat them.

It was a stand-off. He didn't dare approach the creature. Its mouth and teeth were obviously capable and dangerous. On the other hand, it didn't move towards him either. It huddled in a lumpy mass, drawing itself up tighter every time he passed more gas.

His confidence grew as the creature withdrew into a tight ball. Eventually, he summoned up his courage and approached. The thing was forming another shell over its body. Apparently, that was what it did to avoid inhospitable environments.

As Ash watched, the shell thickened. His problem with beans had an unexpected good side. He passed another batch of gas right beside the creature. It didn't move. Perhaps the shell was thick enough to protect it.

It was a long trip back to Luna. Ash kept eating beans despite the associated indigestion and subsequent intestinal pain they brought him. After some thought, he also disconnected the air-scrubber part of the time. He ran it only enough to ensure that he could breathe. The air in the small ship became rank quickly.

The creature's shell thickened and took on its jeweled finish. Ash had picked up the discarded pieces of the first shell and stored them in a box. They could be valuable in and of themselves. They were certainly pretty enough.

He ate beans and waited to arrive. He theorized that it wasn't the organic odor but the methane that the creature disliked. Whatever it was, he didn't want to risk having it attack again, so he kept up his defensive efforts.

Ash's boss was both complimentary and incredulous.

"That was the worst smelling ship I've ever had the misfortune to enter. I don't see how you were able to stand the atmosphere," he said.

Ash replied. "It wasn't a question of wanting to. I had to. Some idiot had loaded the ship with mostly canned beans, and that's nearly all I had to eat. Besides, the alien would probably have eaten me if I had let the air become pure enough for it to re-hatch. I just endured as best I could."

The boss said, "The metals alone will ensure you get a significant bonus, but if we can recover the ship you found, you'll be worth millions. The xenobiologists are agitating to get their hands on the alien, too. We've allowed it to hatch in a secure environment. It seems intelligent, so perhaps there will be some way to communicate with it eventually. Who knows what we'll learn. You've set a record, young man. Your voyage is the most profitable one ever. When are you going back out?"

Ash shook his head negatively. "I'm heading back to Earth as fast as I can. I want to get some decent food, and I intend to stay as far away from beans as possible for the rest of my life."

He didn't mention the pieces of shell that he'd stowed in his personal bag. The creature's second hatching had yielded more shell pieces, and the material had hit the jewelry market like a bolt of lightning. Women were fighting over jewelry created with a piece of alien shell. Ash figured he had enough shell to double his bonus pay.

He was wealthy enough to ensure that Richelle would regret her decision. In retrospect, he was glad she'd dumped him. It had provided the motivation he'd needed to become a prospector.

One thing he'd learned was not to give in to his impulsive nature. In the future, he'd take care to check every ramification of his prospective decisions. There would be no more getting on spaceships that were improperly supplied.

Ash was highly displeased to find that the menu on the shuttle back to Earth included baked beans.

The End

Asterats

I was reading about fragility as it relates to complex systems, and it occurred to me that the way we govern ourselves is one such system. I paired that idea with the problems that currently beset science. The same problems have interfered with science as it has been practiced in the western world since the scientific method was developed. It's subject to the whims of those who hold the purse strings. This problem has dramatically restricted human potential. If science were based on a meritocracy of ideas, humanity would be far advanced beyond our current level. Then I blended the above two ideas with one of our all-time bug-bears: the inability to get along with each other, especially when the other person looks a little different or possibly comes from another tribal group. This story was the result.

It wasn't fair. Dane mulled the situation over in his head for the hundredth time. He'd carefully controlled for all the variables, even some his critics hadn't thought of as yet, and the resonant cavity worked. There was a barely detectable amount of thrust from the apparatus. The physics department chair maintained that his results were due to experimental error since there was no measurable ejected matter.

He grinned wryly. Issac Newton would be spinning in his grave. Moreover, if his theory were anywhere close to what was happening, Einstein would be rolling over too. The device was a success. It was limited, but he was sure he could transform it into a real space drive. It just wasn't fair that he'd lost his grant.

It was all politics, of course. There was significant money invested in solar sails and ionic ejection engines, and corporate lobbyists were working overtime to get the politicians to back one or the other to the detriment of all other parties. Dane's project was merely collateral damage as far as they were concerned.

Dane was a student, not a big name, and his sponsoring professor was considered a crack-pot in the academic physics community. That was partially due to his accepting Dane's ideas as worth investigating. There were numerous academic papers dismissive of the whole idea of what was considered a somewhat magical microwave drive.

Dane's problem had culminated with a commentary by Nobel Prize-winning Professor Fasmu, a highly respected sociologist. Fasmu stated that anyone who thought such a device would work had probably been exposed to too much microwave leakage and inadvertently cooked their brains. The popular press had picked up on that to the point that Dane even had his picture published in one of the corporate news sites with the caption: "Another Brain-damaged Caucasian."

Dane could understand the antecedents of the slur. He knew he was smart and had always thought that would be enough, but there had been a significant component of luck to his admission. In this day and age, most citizens looked down on white men. Caucasians were considered too bound to their cultural background of reason to be rational. That euro-centric tendency toward rationality was held to be responsible for a whole litany of both real and fictional historical sins.

Even so, the picture's caption had hurt, especially since Meredith had dumped him after the article came out. She couldn't risk associating with someone who was considered crazy. It would hurt her academic career.

In the ensuing argument, he'd thoughtlessly pointed out that her academic specialty was of dubious utility to the advancement of humanity. Deconstructing literature and writing about reality as a strictly cultural interpretation, subject to individual whim, didn't seem to be helping anyone as far as he could see. Telling her that had been one of his less well-thought-out ideas.

He'd been careful to avoid getting into an argument with her over her theories. That was because he thought she was beautiful and was hopeful that their relationship would advance beyond casual dating.

He'd been naive. In retrospect, he could see that
Meredith had been using him to impress her friends. She
had gained status because he was supposedly a scientist.
The second and more hurtful reason was that he was one
of the few white males who had made it through the
quota system imposed by the university, and Meredith
had been showing that she was fair-minded enough to
consider him as a possible mate.

Apparently, it had all been a charade. Dane had been
slow to figure it out, so maybe he wasn't as bright as he
thought he was. He tried to point out that history had
become distorted, but she dismissed his argument. She
told him that his race's genetically-caused mental defects
had been the cause of all past inequality. She'd hoped
that he was not that way, but now she could see that he
had the same problem. She could never consider him as a
potential mate. She was embarrassed that she'd ever
allowed herself to be seen in public with him.

He reviewed the sequence of events bitterly. The
international space agency had pulled his grant in part
because of his race. As soon as the article with his picture
appeared, there was a demonstration. Other students had
protested to the dean of academic equality, which had
snowballed into the loss of his grant. It seemed that the
primary intent of funding was to equalize opportunities
and not to reward innovation.

As he mulled the situation over, he finished destroying
the core elements of his apparatus. It was late at night,
and he was due to be evicted from the lab tomorrow.
He'd put too much work into the system to let it fall into
the hands of others, even if they didn't believe it worked.

When he had finished his destruction, all that was left was a useless pile of miscellaneous parts. He'd gone to the effort of mixing in things that had no purpose in his device to make any attempt at reconstruction difficult. Likewise, he'd taken some of the critical components and thrown them into the dumpster behind the social justice department. He'd climbed in and covered the parts with banned books that were being removed from the university library.

Dane had already let his apartment go. He had little money of his own, and now that he'd lost his grant, he would have to apply for public assistance or take whatever menial job was available to him.

He pocketed the USB drive that held the plans for his device and exited the physics building, breaking his key off in the lock as a final symbol of defiance. He was angry and determined to find some way to show everyone that he was right about his invention. Eventually, he remembered Chad.

Chad was an acquaintance who made a living by various unorthodox means, some of which were undoubtedly criminal. Dane had helped the guy with some illicit computer projects and even designed a highly-illegal, short-range EMP weapon. Chad had needed it for something about which Dane didn't want to know. The man was a useful if dangerous resource. Dane feared he would almost certainly end up in rehab with a mind-wipe.

It was a risk hanging around with him, but Chad was one
of the few people who didn't care about Dane's race and
who appreciated his ability with physics. Maybe he
should check in with Chad.

Dane's anger had reached the point that he was willing to
work for Chad, even if the projects were against the law.
He climbed on the autonomous bus, glanced at the face-
recog scanner for his fare, and rode towards the Ribbon
district.

Chad had had his base of operations in an old warehouse
near one edge of the Ribbon. He claimed to be in the
space industry. He had some legitimate contracts to
supply parts and food to various space stations.

Nano-tech had advanced quickly, and the construction of
the Ribbon had made Chad's business possible. The early
space-elevators had been on high mountain peaks near
the equator, making surface transportation difficult.

The Ribbon was new and the first of its kind. It was
composed of diamond nano-tubules rather than carbon.
The stronger material meant that the Ribbon could be
relatively narrow at its base and allowed it to be located at
a northern latitude. It was a kilometer wide, but the fact
that it was only two millimeters thick was the amazing
part. It grew wider as it approached the 35,786-kilometer
level. That was the point of highest centrifugal stress. The
Ribbon narrowed beyond that level since the pull
gradually decreased the closer it got to the supporting
mass that swung at the end of its 155,000-kilometer
length.

Dane's ultimate ambition was to get his prototype engine into space. That was the only place he could test it accurately. He'd previously applied for money to carry it up the Ribbon to the point of zero gravity, often simply called GEO. It was expensive, and he'd been passed over each time he applied. Now he'd lost funding entirely. The thought made his mood sink even lower.

There were several projects currently at GEO that were utterly frivolous. Who cared if poetry composed in zero gravity better expressed social goals? What bureaucrat had the authority and poor judgment to provide funding for poets in residence at the GEO point? It was beyond belief.

There were still a few miles to go. Dane's mind wandered back to the Ribbon itself. It made reaching Earth orbit a trivial task, even though it was still expensive.

Objects launched below GEO would drop behind the Ribbon and fall into low Earth orbit. Satellites that detached higher on the Ribbon would have increased momentum and would move outward. The release point could be calculated to place satellites in any desired orbit.

A launch at the 144,000-kilometer point would have enough velocity to travel all the way to Jupiter. The only problem was getting back. No practical space drive existed, and it looked like none would be invented soon, even with all the lobbying. The world government dedicated the bulk of its spending to righting social issues and supporting citizens who couldn't or wouldn't work.

No one wanted to take a one-way trip out of the solar system, so there had never been a crewed mission launched into interplanetary space, although probes had been launched from the Ribbon.

By this point, Dane had worked himself into such a state of bitterness that he would have volunteered on the instant for a one-way trip away from Earth to any destination.

If only he could figure out how to stow away on one of the climbers with a working prototype, Dane knew he could prove his detractors wrong.

The climbers operated on a set of large rollers that gripped the Ribbon tightly between them. There were strands of carbon nano-tubes spaced at intervals forming electric conductors and giving the Ribbon a striped appearance. The climbers used ground-based power to start the journey. They automatically switched to their built-in solar-powered array at the 40-kilometer level.

The world spacecraft development center was at the first LaGrange point of the Earth-Sun mass system. It seemed a long jump from the 50,630-kilometer launch point on the Ribbon, but it was a comfortable flight for the supply drone. It would be flung outward with enough velocity to reduce the 1.5 million kilometer trip to a moderate inconvenience. It took longer for the Climber to reach GEO than for the drone to get to L1.

Dane shook his head. He had missed his stop while he was gathering wool. He jumped off at the next corner and headed back towards Chad's office. It was in an older warehouse separated from the road by a high fence. Dane stopped at the gate and pushed eight unmarked buttons in a pattern that formed the binary number 68. The gates slid back as the ancient ASCII code for "D" was detected.

Dane walked up to the small office door, opened it, and stopped just inside to look around. A figure came toward him, walking quickly across the broad expanse of concrete floor. It was Chad.

"I see'ya, Bruv! You brain mirked from all d'study?" he joked.

Dane said, "Maybe. Maybe not. They terminated my funds. My only hope is to get into space to continue. Think you can help me get to GEO?"

Chad frowned and said, "Go ta the crux, don' you?" Then he smiled, dropped the street slang for a moment, and added, "I understand. You just been effectively kicked out so some doubtless deserving student can muck up your lab while developing a better way to distribute canned beans or something."

Dane looked down in disgust. There was nothing to say. It was probably true. The provost had made it clear that he thought Dane's research wasn't socially valuable.

Chad continued. "Yeah. I owes ya after that las' job. It turn out good. Your equipment ya made netted me a nice profit. So, that leaves us unequal. Yeah, I got a way to get you up, but you're going to have to be flexible. It won't be comfortable or fun. I don't run a tourist service, ya know, Bruv."

Dane shrugged. "Anything, man. It took forever to get my prototype adjusted. Now I've got the plans on a memory chip. If I can access a metal synthesizer at GEO, I could print the thing in a few minutes."

Chad said, "Yeah. I guess, but that not an option. They keep close track of everyone there. You gots to go farther than GEO. Listen, Bruv, I got a way to get ya direct to L1. Ya'll hav'ta ride a supply pod up, though. Once ya get up, the station big enough for a underground economy. I try to get you in with the L1 Rats. They maybe help, ifs they like you. Ya gots to be careful around them, though."

That was frightening. Dane asked, "L1? I hadn't thought of getting out that far. It'd be a good place to test my prototype, but I probably wouldn't be able to come back to Earth, would I?"

Chad answered, "Yeah, L1, but it's danger. If ya get caught, the corporate cops will either send ya down to prison or maybe worse. I hear they launching some prisoners to Mars. Ya might get there in a few years." He paused, then added, "Or not. Ya right, ya won' be coming back probably. Up for that?"

Dane grimaced. "You make a good case for me going to work in industrial robot repair. My dad always said that would be a good career."

"Yeah, but the effin' things most fix themselves now. C'mon back here, and I show you the supply pod. I'd rather ya get gone quick an' on ya way. I got some very touchy buyers showing up the day after tomorrow. They spooky. If they think anything likely to blow their security, they'll beat out'a here, and I might not live through their exit. Ya can't be here then."

Dane nodded. "I understand. I'm ready to go right now. There's nothing here for me."

***

Dane was squeezed into a small space inside one of the cargo containers, then loaded onto the supply drone piggybacked on Ribbon Climber 4. Riding a crewless vessel made him very uneasy, but it took an enormous amount of money to go up as a tourist, so that wasn't even a remote possibility.

Chad had smuggled him into a pressurized container with a load of food supplies that had to be kept from freezing. Dane soon found out that restriction only meant uncomfortably cold to him. He spent the next three days shivering in a synthetic down sleeping bag.

At least it gave him time to think and plan. He mentally went over his prototype and checked through some of the math in his mind. It would work, but there were some minor tweaks he could make. He developed an ingenious waveguide system that he thought would increase the thrust, so his time wasn't unproductive even though the journey seemed to take forever.

It was a good sign when the gravity hit zero. The climber didn't pause at GEO. It continued right past the GEO station and began descending toward the counterweight at the end of the Ribbon. Dane floated for a while and then gradually drifted to what had been the ceiling of his little space. Earth was now up rather than down.

The ambiance was different. There was a sense of immanence in the background vibration of Climber 4. The descent towards the end of the Ribbon gradually accelerated as the centrifugal force increased. Trying to figure out how long it would take to reach the L1 jump-off point was a distraction, but he was missing too many variables. He didn't know Climber 4's mass for one, so he estimated. After some intricate mental calculations, he decided that it would take at least another twenty-four hours, so he resigned himself to wait.

He was surprised when the drone detached. Either he'd been way off in his estimate, or something was wrong. There was no way of knowing, locked inside the food container. He'd just have to wait and see. At least he wouldn't die from starvation. Cold or running out of O2 would take care of that job.

He shivered miserably, finally falling asleep. He was in the middle of an elaborate dream about polar bears when the drone began maneuvering and woke him. There was a period of unpleasant deceleration followed by some heavy bumps and clanking noises. Then the cargo container jerked, and there was a sensation of gradually increasing weight.

Dane pulled himself up and endured the acceleration. There was a crashing sound as the container slammed off the acceleration track and slid to a stop fully matched with the station's rotation.

Almost immediately, there was a click, and the auxiliary hatch opened to reveal a small figure dressed in cold-hold clothing, complete with a facemask and hood.

"K' dirt-foots, get on. We got only a few minutes to get outa here. They be wanting to get these supplies first, so move it!"

The voice sounded like the speaker was maybe twelve, which would match the size. Dane made an effort to hurry, but he was stiff with the cold. The kid groaned, then said, "Ya got to move fast, dirt-foots. C'mon on. I serious." The kid grabbed Dane's arm and pulled hard.

Dane gradually limbered up and began to move faster. They wound through a large hold full of boxes and miscellaneous equipment, then ducked through an airlock and wound their way through narrow halls that seemed to be descending into the bowels of some underworld.

The gravity, no...Dane corrected himself. The centrifugal force increased, so they must be approaching the outside rim of the rotating station. The area was dimly lit and looked deserted.

"Where are we going?" he asked.

The kid glanced back and said, "So, the dirt-foots can talk after all. We going down to the rat warren. The corps stay up in the low G zones. Better shielding, and they like the ease of movement. We only have to watch for patrol drones. You can hear them coming, so they avoidable. Now shut it and c'mon. If they catch ya, it's the macerator or maybe a one-way tour to Jupiter if they ready to try another propulsion system."

That didn't sound good, but Dane ignored the implications and asked, "Why are you here? Chad said he had resources up here, people who would help me."

The answer was brief: "That's me for now. My job to get you safe. What you do after is up to you. Enough talk. C'mon."

Dane was dumped in a room, and the kid disappeared. A burly man came in almost immediately.

"You must be the physics genius Chad told us about," he said. "I hope you're able to learn quick. There's a lot to know and not much time to waste. If ya don't learn quick, ya might as well not have come. We don' need no useless eaters."

He launched into a lecture without waiting for Dane to answer.

The rat warren was in the space between the legitimately occupied central areas of the station and the outside rim. The spent cargo containers were transferred outside and attached to the large structure where they formed storage rooms. They were constructed to be occupied and were cleverly designed to interlock in various ways so the station could grow.

It had been in operation for years now, and thousands of containers were linked together into a rotating cylindrical shape almost five kilometers in length. The rat warren covered a large percentage of the undesirable high-G space and housed a few hundred people.

Up above, there were over thirty thousand corporate employees. The burly man called them "corps." They lived in the low G sections. The elite corps were involved with propulsion research for space drives. Then there were their families, admin staff, service staff, and a small military detachment to maintain order.

The warren was the home of the L1-Rats. They had started as construction workers. Many still legitimately worked on station expansion and maintenance. Their ranks had been augmented by malcontents, injured staff who could no longer work, and older people deemed non-productive. They lived a tenuous life in between the walls. They weren't supposed to be there, but the corps found them occasionally useful and mostly left them alone. Even their raids on supplies were tolerated as long as they didn't take too much.

Dane asked, "What happens if a...uh, a drone patrol catches you?"

The burly man grimaced. "Generally taser ya, and then ya get picked up and taken to the low-G area for disposal. If they need someone to crew an experimental ship, you might get a one-way trip to Jupiter. Not many get the chance to starve to death on the way. They mostly just dump you into the garbage macerator. That's probably more humane. They recycle everything up here. No one sent back to Earth. Too costly. Ya took a one-way trip, dirt-foots. Ya gotta make the best of it."

Dane didn't like the guy's attitude much, but it was helpful information. He said, "I got a 3-d plan I need to print and a load of parts to get. I've got some digital coins as long as things aren't too expensive. I intend to make the best of it as you say."

The man nodded approvingly. "We can get ya access to a 3-d fabber, no prob. We use 'em all the time for station parts. If we can't fab the things ya need, we can probably lift them somewhere. That'll cost ya. Food and water cost more, 'less ya don't eat, dirt-foots."

Dane nodded and asked, "What the eff' is this dirt-foots thing you keep calling me?"

"Dirt-foots! Dirt-foots! Plain to see ya got dirt on ya feet. There's people here that ain't never seen anything but hull plates. They won't like ya much. You cutting into their air, their water, their food, and their space. I hope ya got enough physics to make a difference. We all tired of this life and want more. Ya better be able to help the way Chad said ya could."

Dane did his best to adjust. The drone patrol units were noisy and easy to avoid as long as they were moving. The drones would sometimes sit silently in wait in a corridor. Everyone carried inspection mirrors on extendable handles and used them to look around corners before proceeding. It made for slow progress. For the most part, that was in the lower-G areas nearer the corp areas in the station's center. There was an electronic drone warning system in place in the warren so that people could move freely there.

Dane found out that Burly's real name was James and that he was the nominal chief of the Rats. Dane's carefully hoarded block-chain tokens were eagerly accepted and were enough to allow him to have a combination lab and sleeping unit to himself.

The 3-d plans were in production before his first 12 hour day had passed. The printer operator accepted a small bribe to slip Dane's job in between corp-ordered production runs. The other parts he needed were more complex and posed a more significant problem.

Dane was trying to make a circuit-board fit through an opening in the assembly that had just come off the 3-d printer. The access hole wasn't quite large enough for the board, and it was causing him no end of trouble. His neck was painfully twisted as he tried to see what was causing the hang-up, and his temper had reached the breaking point.

"Hey, dirt-foots, whatcha doin' there?"

He recognized the voice. It was the kid who had first met him. Without looking up, he snapped, "Working! Leave me alone."

The voice said, "Guess ya don want these heavy-duty transformers ya asked for after all, huh?"

Dane straightened out, striking his forehead painfully on a protruding part of the engine.

"Damn it..." he started, then his mouth dropped open in astonishment.

After a bit, he stuttered, "You, you're a girl."

She looked disgusted. "What did ya think I was Dirt-foots? Ya supposed to be some scientist, but ya don't seem too smart. Are you sure you know what you're doing?"

She had gradually dropped the street talk. She probably wasn't trying to make friends with him. It seemed more likely that she was well educated and used jargon as a defense.

Dane recovered himself a bit at that thought. He inspected her more closely and decided that she was beautiful, even if her hair was cut short for pressure suit reasons. He sighed. Her skin was far darker than his. Her features were regular and delicate. He'd be lucky to get the time of day from her if she wasn't delivering the parts he had told James he needed.

"Uh, yeah. I guess you could say I'm a scientist. I didn't get my degree, but I know what I'm doing," he said. It sounded lame, and her semi-sneer made him regret his lack of social skills.

She sniffed and looked mildly amused. "Here's your transformers." She waved her hand back, indicating a self-powered flatbed cart following her.

He said, "Great, I'm almost ready for them. Do you know if anyone has figured out what I can use as a test platform?"

Her face sobered, and she looked at him as if she were seriously evaluating his sanity.

"Look, I know you're new here, dirt--" She stopped herself and then started over. "I know you don't know what's going on here, but there isn't time for a leisurely test. First, if your engine is successful and the corps find out about it, you'll be lucky if they don't instantly space you without a suit. They'll most certainly destroy your engine. Too much money is backing what they're doing, even though it isn't going to work. There's too much at stake in dot.gov subsidies. They'll never risk their funding. They're going to keep right on sucking up tax credits, and the longer they can drag this out, the better for them."

Dane hadn't thought of the political situation, but it made sense. Corporate lawyers created most legislation and specifically designed it for corporations. Lobbyists were hired to convince elected officials to sponsor bills and ensure they became law. Everyone benefited but the ordinary people. Some big money was being spent on this installation, even though it was trivial compared to total global spending.

She cleared her throat to get his attention. "Second, and most important from my position, is the corps have recently decided that they don't want to put up with us Rats. Despite the services we provide, they've decided that we're net consumers who don't pay our way. They're starting to deploy killer drone swarms. They don't have too many of the things right now, but they're working on making more. It's practically impossible to defend against them, so we need to get the Hell off this station fast."

Dane nodded. He knew something about killer drone technology. The small drones could go almost anywhere and were designed to fire a shaped charge into humans.

They'd usually go for the brain, but the heart was also a good target, as was the throat. There was no dodging since they had reaction times that humans couldn't match. Even swinging a large net or a tennis racquet was only partially effective. The drones were expendable. One shot per drone. The explosion would destroy both the drone and its target.

He glanced down at his engine, then at her face. He caught her unguarded expression, and it was one of worry blended with hope. Hope, he realized, in him or at least in his invention.

Her expression flipped instantly back to a bored look, but he took the opportunity to explain a little about his engine.

"This will work. I've made some rather startling advances in efficiency. The original resonant cavity drive idea has been around for a long time. It was first proposed in 2001 by Shawyer. No respectable physicist would give it any credibility since it seemed to violate all the laws of physics as they were known at the time. There just couldn't be any thrust since nothing came out of the drive."

She interrupted, "Yeah. I'm not an idiot. Action equals reaction. So what have you done that's so great?"

He grinned. The girl was more educated than she let on.

He continued. "The thing is, no one was sure about the quantum vacuum. It was theorized that it was full of virtual particles, but there was no good evidence that it could react with ordinary matter, except in some odd conceptions of gravity. The resonant cavity just bounces microwaves back and forth in a shaped chamber. Nothing escapes. Nothing that is, but virtual quantum particles in the zero-point field are given some momentum by the microwaves. The particles are undetectable, so it looks like nothing is coming out, but there is a definite effect. The engine creates thrust. Maybe it's only a tiny bit of thrust, but it's more than a large light sail can generate."

"So, you're saying Shawyer's idea works. How efficient is it, and what did you do to increase efficiency?" she asked.

Dane was beginning to like this girl. Not only was she beautiful, but she was smart, too. He had almost forgiven her for their original interaction.

"Shawyer used a frustrum: a truncated cone. That made for more thrust at the large end. There were other slightly different designs, too. What I did was to provide a conical focusing device inside the frustrum. It bounces the microwaves over to the sides of the structure and into tuned waveguides. The reflected waves are caught and sent back to the narrow end, where the magnetron repowers them to be directed back towards the wide end. That way, even though there is still some reverse thrust due to quantum interaction, it's minimized. My design is roughly three hundred percent more efficient. The thrust, if my calculations are correct, is enough to propel a ship to Mars within about fifteen days."

She exclaimed, "Fifteen! Why that's impossible."

He nodded. "Yeah, that's what everyone says. I don't think so. The momentum builds up rather quickly. Of course, you have to allow for turn-around and deceleration. Otherwise, you're going to exit the solar system."

She looked as if she was concentrating intensely. It gave her a vulnerable air, so Dane gathered his courage and asked, "You never said. What's your name?"

She jerked, then looked him up and down for a moment. She answered, "I guess you're okay. You can call me Tiff. I know you're Dane."

She hesitated, then continued. "So why are you here? I mean, well, here instead of at some university or maybe a corporation?"

Dane answered, "Two reasons. First, I'm one a minority. You might have noticed my skin is the wrong color. Second, no one believes my calculations. They told me that my math was wrong and that I should never have been allowed to work on my idea. The implication was that I wasn't smart enough to know not to pursue the impossible. I'm here to prove they're wrong."

He looked down at the equipment he was trying to assemble. "I thought if I could demonstrate that my engine worked, then they'd have to admit I was correct. I'm just glad that your people are giving me a chance."

Tiff said, "Okay, dirt-foots, you don't know anything about us Rats. To start, I don't care what color your skin is. Nobody up here does. You bleed red, don't you?"

She looked up towards the center of the station. "Well, the corps up there in the light gravity care about your skin color, but we're the Rats. What we have is what you might call a meritocracy. You're as good as you can do. If you help us survive, you can be black, blue, white, green, or puce and no one will care. If you're lying and don't deliver, well, people will be angry. No one likes to have her hopes raised based on a lie."

She'd unconsciously slipped into a personal mode of speech. Dane caught her gaze and looked directly into her eyes. They were large and brown and so attractive that he almost forgot what he was going to say. With a guilty start, he said, "I'm confident this will work. I just need those transformers and a space-worthy vessel to use for a test."

Tiff frowned. "You forgot what I said. You are not going to get a test. We've got a large section of this station ready to detach. You know each supply module is like a ship, right. Well, we've got a block of eighty modules hooked up with explosive bolts. They're supplied and have their own power. We grabbed one of the spare reactors out of storage and also a bunch of solar panels. You'll have plenty of electricity."

Dane felt the blood rush from his face. "You mean you all are going to get in this, this improvised ship and hope that my engine can fly us away from here?"

"Yes. That is exactly what we're going to do. If you don't get us out of here in less than maybe seventy-two hours, we probably won't survive."

He asked, "What's to prevent the corps from simply shooting a missile at us once we break away?"

She laughed rather grimly. "That's not a problem. They have a few missiles, but one of our people is a missile expert and does the maintenance. He'd be welcomed if he wanted to live up there, but he's got a wife who was injured, and she wouldn't be. He's fixed the missile guidance so that they'll fly out and then circle back to the station. If they shoot at us, they'll end up blowing a hole in themselves."

Dane felt that was extreme. "What about the innocents that may be affected? Aren't there any children or pregnant women in the low gravity area?"

She shrugged. "No. We're all on birth control. There's too much radiation up here to risk conceiving. No kids to worry about, and every single corp-rat is against us. Don't worry about it. They've decided they want us dead. If they kill themselves, Earth will just have to start with a new L1 station."

Something else occurred to Dane. "If we are successful—I mean, if my engine flies us out of here, where will we go?"

"Isn't it obvious?" she asked. "We'll head for the asteroid zone. There are plenty of resources there. We can make more of your engines and see if we can create our own civilization. We'll change from L1-Rats to asteroid Rats."

It took twenty hours. Dane had finished his assembly shortly after Tiff had brought him the transformers, but he checked and cross-checked the circuits and connections. He took a third set of measurements of the frustrum just to make sure everything was in its correct place. Finally, he called for James.

James came through the door, nearly brushing both sides with his thick shoulders. Several other people filtered in that Dane hadn't previously met. Tiff slipped through the door last and stood near the exit.

Dane didn't wait. "I'm ready. As ready as I'll ever be. I'm sure my engine will work. I've calculated the mass we're going to be pushing as best I can, and I'm afraid the acceleration is going to be slower than I'd initially thought."

One of the older men said, "We didn't tell you everything. We've got the explosives set to give us a hard shove away from the main station mass. We'll time it so that we're headed for Mars orbit when we blow the bolts, and then you can turn on your engine. The initial explosion will give us a boost. We'll move away from L1 pretty quickly."

Dane wiped his face with his hand. "Well, yes, but that doesn't change the acceleration factor for my engine. I'll have to recalculate everything again once we figure out how fast we're moving away." He looked at the man and asked, "Did you calculate our velocity based on the amount of explosives?"

The man looked at James. "Uh, no. There are complicating factors. We're not quite sure. We'll just have to wait until we separate to see."

James asked, "As I understand it, your drive doesn't have to be located anywhere in particular so that it is pointing the right way. Right?"

"I'd like to have it at the end of the ship. It would make steering more manageable, and besides, there's a small amount of thrust attenuation if the virtual particles have to pass through much matter. We'll do better if it's at the back.

James grinned. "Good. That's where it's located right now. This compartment is at the end of the pods we've set to separate. Now, how are you going to steer the thing?"

Dane pointed and said, "I've mounted it on gimbals. Computer-controlled with very accurate servos. We can change direction in small increments. The system is capable of moving from degrees down through minutes to seconds. I think we can keep it pushing us in the direction we want."

James said, "The asteroid belt is where we want to be. There are plenty of resources out there. We've decided that Ceres should be our initial destination. We'll reconfigure the ship into multiple vessels when we get there and provide each with a copy of your drive. Then we set up our own habitat."

A continuous beeping warning stopped the discussion.

James shouted, "Drone alert. Lock everything down. Now!" He grabbed his comm unit and gave a set of commands. Listened to the response, then looked at Dane.

"We've got to launch right now. There's been a Kessler event. The Ribbon was severed right at GEO by a perfect storm of cascading satellite parts. It wasn't supposed to be possible. The structure was designed to be immune to normal debris strikes, but this one wasn't normal. The Ribbon broke, and the counterweight is headed in this direction. The corps up above are panicking. They've decided to get rid of us immediately to preserve their supplies and air. We're under attack, so we blow the bolts and separate before the drones can get into our space."

He said something into the comm unit. There was a pause; then a rumble shuddered through the station's structure. The pod's apparent gravity instantly changed directions, causing the humans to fall and slide against one wall. Dane found himself partially suspended, hanging from his engine mount.

There was a buzzing sound, and three small drones came through the still opened door. The devices shot forward and exploded against three of the humans. The smell of explosives and blood filled the chamber.

James had regained his feet and was shouting into the comm unit. After a bit, he said, "Clean up the mess. Those were the only kill-bots that got into this section. We've lost about a hundred people total, but we are now totally separate from the main L1 station. The corps can fry in Hell."

Dane had worked his way around to a sitting position that gave him access to the computer he'd built into the drive system. He set it to some calculations, then said, "Hell is where they're going. My system interfaces with our radar unit, and they've been knocked out of the L1 position. They're headed towards low earth orbit. If the Earth doesn't suck them in, they'll make a slingshot pass around the planet and then head directly toward the Sun."

Tiff shouted, an incoherent cry that was midway between relief and agony.

James shook his head, then said, "They've got their hands full. I doubt they'll shoot at us. Dane, get your engine ready to go. We'll have the modules reconfigured into a line in an hour. Then let's get out of here."

Dane said, "Well, I guess I'm ready to take a test run."

Tiff interjected, "I told you. No test. This is it. Your engine better work."

He looked at her. Her eyes were shining with something, but he couldn't tell if she was angry or afraid. "I'm sure it will work," he said.

There was a series of clangs, followed by booming noises. James said, "The modules are aligning themselves now. We'll be ready shortly."

The Rats worked like fury to adjust the shape of the structure, and it gradually began to look like a space vessel rather than a curved arc of cargo modules.

Dane was given the signal and turned on his engine. It made a slight humming noise, but that was all. It was vaguely anticlimactic.

Tiff looked at him questioningly. "Is it working?" she asked.

Dane was bent over the computer, concentrating, then he raised his head, triumph in his eyes. "Yes. It's adding to our acceleration. I've calculated the vector for Ceres. Starting at our present speed and allowing for the drive acceleration, we'll reach turn-around in a hundred and twenty-four hours."

When they were a little over three thousand kilometers away from the erratically spinning bulk of the L1 station, they detected multiple missile launches. The corp rats were trying to take revenge, futile though it might be.

None of the missiles struck the Rat's ship. They all looped around, passing through the L1 point, and then continued accelerating off in random directions. One of the missiles happened to be on the exact vector that the remaining part of the L1 station was following. It exploded against the bulk of the mass, but the Rats paid no attention. The L1 station was no longer a part of their lives.

Tiff came into what was now called the Engine room with a tray. "Captain James told me to bring you some food. We're nearly ready to connect internal controls so you can come to the control room at the front of the ship. You'll be able to steer from there."

She paused and looked embarrassed." Dane, I owe you an apology. At first, I didn't like you. I thought you were a fraud. I didn't think you could do it. But you did. I made a big production about this being a meritocracy, but I had my own doubts. I've been searching through my beliefs since your engine started working. I've concluded that I was at least a little prejudiced. I was wrong, and I'm sorry."

She moved closer to him, leaning forward due to her decreased weight in the acceleration. Whether by accident or by intent, their lips met, and then her arms came around his shoulders. He kissed her back for a moment.

She leaned back, her eyes wide. "That was very nice," she said. "Let's do it again."

He was only too happy to oblige.

There was a noise at the door and the two guiltily separated.

James stood there, steadying himself against the door frame. "Don't stop on my account. I just wanted to congratulate Dane. We'll be at turn-around for Ceres in another twelve hours."

They looked at each other, and Dane pulled Tiff closer. She didn't resist.

James added, "We'll set up a base there. The first thing we're going to do is explore a nearby asteroid. It's not very large, but we've been watching it. One of our older guys was a geologist before he left Earth. He's run some calculations, and I had one of our engineers cross-check them."

Dane asked, "What did they show?"

James laughed aloud. "That's the critical question. The asteroid is too small to see from Earth, but it has a high density. Based on its estimated size, it could be composed of one or a combination of several heavy metals, but I'm betting the thing is at least partially loaded with gold. We estimate about a hundred million tons of it."

Dane hugged Tiff tightly while his mind whirled. Dane opened his mouth, but before he could speak, Tiff asked, "Wouldn't that make us, I mean our colony, more valuable than the whole of Earth?"

James said, "Well, it would ruin the value of gold if we transported it all at once to Earth, but if we're careful, we should be able to negotiate for supplies with small amounts. We'll have to make sure they don't know where we're getting it. If they found out, they'd try to take it away from us, and if they couldn't do that, they'd attempt to destroy it."

Dane said, "We should have plenty of time to get established. I didn't record my changes to the resonant cavity idea. In fact, the main innovation I made, the most effective one, I came up with on the way to L1. We're the only people who have that secret. The physics department at the university knows I was working on a space drive, but even if they start now, it should take them years to duplicate my work, and that's if they get lucky and guess what I've done. Besides, they're all geared up for various reaction drives, none of which have been successful. The government might make it out here in about five years or so, but that's also assuming they change their spending priorities and devote more money to research. I don't think the population will be happy about that decision.."

Tiff added, "By then, we'll have plenty of ships and will have established ourselves. The asteroid belt is ours."

James said, "We are even safer than you think. If they show signs of aggression towards us, we can simply threaten to push a few thousand tons of gold into low earth orbit. They'll go crazy trying to reach it. The best part is that it will crash the global economy if it gets to the surface. If we have to, we can make sure that chunks fall all over the place. The current government won't survive the currency devaluation and ensuing uproar."

Tiff laughed with joy, then said, "I think we've graduated from Li-Rats to Asteroid Rats."

Dane added, "Rats with golden teeth. Maybe we should call ourselves Aste-Rats.

She kissed him again. "I know one Aste-Rat that I'm going to be living with for a long time. James, you're the Captain. You can marry us, can't you?"

James' teeth showed in a bright grin. "Yes, I guess that's part of my authority.

The End

TEOTW

This story also originated with my heart problems. I studied the human heart intensively to try and understand what was happening inside me. It may surprise you to know that if you have a group of people stand in a circle and hold hands, then have the people at each end of the line hold the leads to an EKG recorder, the wave you record will be the summation of the heartbeats of everyone in the line. We're far more connected than we commonly realize.

The radio was set to an oldies station when it happened. It was playing a song from 1987 by R.E.M. to a frantic puppy. The puppy was in a bedroom with pink walls. He was sitting on a canopy bed with pink ruffles. The pillows on the bed were decorated with gaudy pictures of princesses. One of the walls had black handwritten slogans and poorly composed versions of popular thoughts and memes written in a flourishing hand. The room seemed like a warm, friendly place, and it was an unlikely scene for the peaceful but grim event that had just occurred.

What happened in that room also happened across the face of the globe. It was terrible, and yet, it was actually kind of funny. It was so mundane in nature, yet it had such an impact.

It was the Armageddon event that no one had predicted. Instead of a flash of fire, a wave of icy cold, an earthquake, a tidal wave, an asteroid killer smashing into the center of downtown, the sun exploding, everything just ended without a sound.

No one could have precisely predicted which event would be the proximal cause. In retrospect, it might have been something significant such as a sudden increase in field strength caused by a distant astronomical event. It might have been something small such as the Rothstein's teenager turning on her new cell phone for the first time. One moment she was lying on her bed deliciously anticipating conversing with her soon-to-be awestruck friends about all of the functions of her new phone, and the next, those fleeting moments of joyful thought were gone for good.

No one knew what had happened. There was no one left who cared or could comprehend that things were now different. No one, that is, except her little dog, who couldn't understand why she had stopped moving.

What is a field? No, not in the farming sense, but in the sense meant by physicists. Even physicists aren't exactly sure. Of course, the math describes the field, but does it actually explain its origin? Of course not. What is an electron? Well, yeah, it's a sub-atomic particle, and it has a negative charge, but what exactly is a negative charge? The name isn't the thing; the map isn't the territory.

Fields have unusual properties. The three-dimensional sphere of a field expands from its point of origin and extends into space, moving at the speed of light. It has the potential to continue on to infinity or, at least, to the farthest reaches of the Universe, weakened, perhaps, but still in its proper form.

Fields don't suddenly disappear at some given distance from their source. In theory, they have the potential to reach across the Universe. Take any star, for example. Its electromagnetic field will extend 186,000 miles in all directions in one second. The field has extended almost 6 trillion miles away from the center point in one year.

Given the estimated age of the Universe as 13 or 14 billion years and the fact that it contains untold billions of galaxies and untold billions of smaller objects, and each object has its own gravitational field, and all these fields overlap, we have billions of billions of billions of overlapping fields impinging upon our bodies.

Of course, there are other sources of fields. Think of the electromagnetic fields that surround electrical appliances or that are emitted by our communication devices. Humans don't usually sense these fields. The fact that our bodies are interpenetrated by millions of phone calls, radio programs, television shows, and many, many other signals passes unnoticed by the vast majority of people. Still, it is just as true as if they actually noticed or cared.

Then there are bio-energetic fields. The human heart has its own field. It's the strongest field emitted by the human body. It's over one thousand times bigger than the magnetic field of the human brain. Every time the heartbeats, it generates electrical charges that expand into a roughly egg-shaped field.

A typical EKG shows a P wave which is the pulse from the atria. The P wave is followed by another sharp wave called the R spike caused by the contraction of the heart's ventricles. The Q and S waves bracket the R spike. Every cell in our bodies is bathed in the fields from the heart. If you measure carefully, you can even find the heart's field reflected in a person's brain waves.

It has been shown that our heart fields impact other people. This effect is measurable when we are near each other. We may not be aware of it, but we are touched by the heartbeat of all living creatures since fields have an infinite range.

Let's change our focus for a moment. Think of a common audio device: the sound-masking head-phone. These are convenient for people in noisy environments. Such a head-phone set contains a microphone and circuitry that samples the external noise and then creates a continuous sound that is one hundred and eighty degrees out of phase with the external noise. This masks out the external sounds, and it is as if the listener were in a quiet environment. The device depends on the fact that waves can cancel each other just as fields can interfere with each other.

Back to the pink room. Regardless of the actual triggering event, the result was that the additive sums of all of the fields on the instant of 5:05:36 PM Eastern Standard Time on July the 3rd, 2012, suddenly formed a short-lasting but intense counter-pulse which damped the heart fields of all living humans. After ten seconds of amazed wonder about why they had suddenly fallen to the ground, everyone died. Yes. Everyone.

Most other primates, some mammals, and all birds died also. Smaller dogs survived along with all amphibians, reptiles, fish, and insects.

After the event, the field strength faded as human artifacts gradually lost power and failed. The Earth was ready for the next dominant life form.

At 5:05:55 PM Eastern Standard Time on July the 3rd, 2012, the little puppy began to howl in grief-stricken tones just as the radio was finishing the song by R.E.M.

The puppy didn't understand the irony of the chorus: "... It's the end of the world as I know it..."

The End

Hattie

This story is woven into my first trilogy. Hazel is a character in that series. When I was writing Confederation, I originally thought she was going to have a bit part, but

she turned out to be such a strong person, that I felt she deserved more attention. If my plans go well (they never do), I'll probably write a book featuring her as the main character. In any event, be prepared, she's tough (and don't say I didn't warn you.)

The Mother-effers were coming again. Hazel had been doing her best to avoid the soldiers for the last week. She'd been hiding in a dry, concrete culvert that went under the narrow, asphalt road a mile from the remains of her parent's farm.

Hazel had been in shock for the first three days, but now her emotions were beginning to crystallize. Physical discomfort and hunger seemed to increase the effect, and now she was experiencing nothing but cold, hard anger.

Last Saturday had been bright and sunny. She'd been gathering eggs when her dad had come running around the barn shouting for her to hide. Soldiers were coming. There had been smoke from burning farms in the distance for the last twenty-four hours, and she and her parents had realized that something terrible was coming. Now it had arrived.

Last night, over supper, they'd argued. She had wanted to run, but her parents were adamant that they had to stay with the farm.

"Hattie, the animals need us. They won't be able to survive alone," her father reasoned, calling her by her nickname. "Besides, if it is His will that they come here and find us, then nothing we can do will change that."

She wished that her parents weren't so religious. Since society stopped years ago, their faith had only grown deeper and firmer. Now, they wouldn't leave, and she knew they'd take no steps to defend themselves. "Turn the other cheek," her father always said.

Her mother added, "The cows have to be milked twice a day; otherwise, they may get udder rot. We owe it to them to stay. They've supported us well in the past, and we need them, too."

They'd made it clear, though, that if armed men found them, she was to hide. Her father and mother looked at each other with worry in their eyes, and then her mother had said, "Hazel, you're too pretty to take any chances with invaders. They would probably kidnap you, and you might be seriously hurt."

Hazel knew what they were talking about. "You mean they'd rape me, don't you. You needn't think I'm totally ignorant. I'm nearly an adult," she fumed.

Her parents looked shocked. That had pretty much been the end of the discussion. Her mother went into the sitting room to read her bible by candlelight, and her dad went out to the barn to repair something or other. Things were always breaking.

Two weeks ago, a refugee family had come by the farm. They were headed for the mountains, the distant mountains. They hadn't seen any soldiers, but they'd heard tales of atrocities, and that was enough to drive them towards safety.

Hazel had only dreamed about the mountains. She'd never seen more than a faint purple line against the western sky. Before the EMP blast, back when she was still a child, her parents had told her that they'd take a vacation to the front range, but it never happened. They never made enough money on their small farm since it was barely a subsistence-level enterprise. They always had enough to eat, but there was precious little left over for clothes, let alone luxuries like vacations or even birthday or Christmas presents.

She'd gone to school in the small town that was eighteen miles to the south, and that was just about the limit of her exposure to the outside world. That and reading. There hadn't been any school since the EMP burst, and she'd read and re-read every book in the house.

She had turned sixteen three months ago. In her heart, she had harbored dreams of a life that had more in it than gathering eggs.

At her dad's shout, she'd put the egg basket up against the side of the chicken coop and dashed off into the cornfield to the west of the house. There was a drainage ditch on the far side of the field, and she made her way to it. Once there, she scrambled down into the dry ditch and waited, hoping her parents would show up.

There was a rustling in the corn. Hazel peered over the edge of the ditch in trepidation, wondering if the soldiers had followed her or if it was her parents. Shortly a black and tan muzzle came through the corn. It was Katie, their aged border collie.

She snapped her fingers, and the dog came over to the ditch, wagging her tail. It took some pulling and lifting on her part, but she got Katie down over the edge. The old dog was so stiff that she couldn't jump or scramble down easily.

It was hot, and there was only a slight breeze. They sat in the ditch listening to the insects buzzing in the corn, waiting.

Suddenly there were two shots, then three, and then after a pause, a fourth echoed over the cornfield. Katie whimpered.

Hazel could hear men shouting off in the distance towards the farmhouse. She waited for a few minutes, wondering what to do. Her mind was abruptly made up for her when she saw a column of black smoke rising from across the field. Then she heard the squealing of their pig, Blackie. She'd named him in jest since he was a white-colored animal.

His squealing rose in terror and then abruptly faded in a gurgling sound. She'd seen hogs butchered before, and this sounded like he'd just had his throat cut. She thought about creeping through the corn to see what was happening, but a sudden cold fear came over her, and she turned resolutely and followed the ditch down towards the culvert, taking care not to leave any footprints where the dust had blown up into thick, soft patches.

She took the dog into the culvert, and they huddled behind a bunch of dried weeds that blocked the narrow tube. She'd had to push her way past the weeds, forcing the dog ahead of her and checking carefully for snakes as they entered. Once inside, another blockage of debris and weeds provided shelter from the other end.

She carefully crawled back to the entrance and backed in, brushing out the signs of their entry with a piece of tumbleweed. Then she and Katie lay on the dry sand and kept quiet. After an hour or so, a group of men came down the road and walked over the culvert. She could hear them talking as they walked.

One said in a loud voice, "Pretty poor pickins at that last place, not even nothin' much worth stealing, stupid sumbitches."

He was answered by another who spoke more quietly, "Yeah, but we got some good bacon, and that woman wasn't too bad either. Too bad for her that she had to fight so much."

Loud-mouth came back with, "Did ya see that stupid farmer. Imagine him trying to fight us with a pitchfork."

Another added, "He looked pretty surprised with that hole through his head."

Hazel sniffled and tried to suppress a sob by biting her lip. Nevertheless, one of the men said, "Say, there was some smaller-sized dresses in the second bedroom. There might'a been a girl lived there. D'ya think we'd better look under the road here?"

She quivered in terror and held her hand on Katie's muzzle to suppress a possible snarl or bark. There was a scrambling sound as the men came off the roadway and bent down to peer into the culvert.

"Na, there's nothing in here but a bunch of weeds and crap," Loud-mouth shouted. "It's so plugged that ya can't see through. No tracks going in, either."

Hazel was glad that she'd taken the time to blur the signs of her passage, erasing their tracks. She quivered in an agony of fear that one of them would try to crawl in and discover her hide-out.

"Hey, Tim, get yer ass down here and look in this here hole," shouted Loud-mouth.

There was another scrambling sound, and someone said, "It's pretty plugged."

Loud-mouth said, "Why don't ya slide in there and see what's what?" He seemed to have only one volume setting for his voice. Hattie couldn't see him, but she imagined that he was fat and filthy.

Tim answered with a tone of disgust, "Whyn't you? It's too damned tight for a man to go in that hole. An 'sides, there might be a rattler or two in there. I ain't a goin' a do it."

Loud-mouth cursed, and Tim called him a 'Damned fool.' There was the sound of a little scuffle, and Loud-mouth grunted as if he'd been struck in the stomach, then said, "I'll get you for that someday, you sumbitch."

Tim replied, "Maybe, but I ain't waiting down here for it. I'm going to catch up with the rest of the guys."

There were some more scrambling noises as they crawled back up onto the road, and then all was quiet.

She remained still until dark when thirst drove her and the dog out and back to the farm.

It hadn't been a good day, and it became far worse when they reached the farmstead.

She now thought of herself as Hattie. In her mind, she was Hazel no longer. That was another person who'd lived in another time. Hattie was a stronger name, someone who didn't feel grief, someone who survived, and most especially, someone who lived for revenge.

She wore a pair of her father's overalls. The legs had been cut off at ankle length, and the suspenders were cinched up to the max. A couple of tee shirts covered by a baggy sweatshirt camouflaged the fact that she had breasts. She'd chopped her ponytail off, and now her hair hung in a ragged mop that could have been a boy's.

A belt around her waist carried her Dad's hunting knife, a butcher knife in an improvised sheath, the small hatchet, and the twenty-two Ruger pistol. It was a nine-shot, semi-automatic covered with rust, but it was deadly accurate and always hit where she pointed it, as several rabbits had found out to their disadvantage.

She was very careful when she approached the culvert, stopping and inspecting the ground for signs of an invader and ensuring that she left no track of her own.

She was alone now. Katie had quietly died the second night they were in the culvert. Perhaps it was just old age, or perhaps the dog felt as much grief at the loss of her family as Hattie did. Either way, it didn't make any difference. When Hattie woke up, Katie was stiff, and her body was cold.

She'd dragged the last member of her family into the cornfield to bury. Then thinking better of it, she'd carried the dog into the farmyard and left her body to decompose behind the barn. There were dog dishes and food on the remains of the porch, and the dog's absence might make an enemy suspicious. Better to just let nature take its course.

By now, the crows and other birds had been at the bodies. Hattie wanted to bury her parents, but the same consideration held. The act of burying implied survivors, and survivors meant there was someone to hunt. She didn't want to send that message.

She'd been lucky to find the pistol hidden in the tin box under the floorboards. Her Dad hadn't believed in guns, but for some reason, he had hidden the small pistol and three boxes of long-rifle ammo along with the deed to the farm. The box had also contained her parent's marriage certificate, two hundred dollars in paper money, some older silver coins, and three gold coins.

The paper money wouldn't buy much. She knew from hearing her parents talk that the only thing most people would take were silver coins. Nevertheless, she carefully hid the box under a rock at the edge of the field. She'd keep the marriage certificate in remembrance.

The deed to the farm had no meaning in this world. Things belonged to those who were strong enough to take and hold them. That was an obvious truth to her. Her parents hadn't been strong enough.

She'd hidden through two additional incursions of the Motherland Army. The last time they'd been in the farmyard, there had been a lot of cursing about the fact that the place was already stripped. One of the ragged men had gone on about how big a mistake it had been for him to join the Motherland Army and ended by calling it the 'Mother-effin' waste.'

Hattie thought that was far more appropriate. Motherland somehow had the connotation of a desirable thing. The army she'd seen was in no way desirable or admirable. She was dead set on staying out of their hands, and their appearance reinforced that desire. She had no delusions about what would happen to her if she were captured.

She was lurking just inside the edge of the cornfield watching the mostly burned-out house. She'd seen a small group of men heading down the road towards the homestead, and she'd finally decided that she was ready for revenge.

Today's group of self-styled soldiers was coming down the road. There were just three of them, walking cautiously along, keeping a close look-out for trouble. They rounded the barn and immediately took to cursing, just like the last group.

"Damn it! Some greedy SOB has already taken this place down. There ain't nothin' here worth the walk," said the apparent leader.

His nearest companion added, "Looks like two dead homesteaders here. Woman over there probably put up a fight, or they'd a taken her with them."

The leader responded, "Maybe, less she wasn't pretty enough. I'd as soon shoot an ugly one as have to listen to 'er complaints."

The third turned with a laugh and said, "You'd shoot her alright, but what gun would ya use?"

They all laughed at that.

Hattie didn't laugh. She was aiming the little Ruger at the leader.

The pistol snapped viciously, and the leader grunted and then said slowly, "What?"

He opened his mouth again, and a stream of blood ran out over his beard. He slowly put his hand on his chest and then toppled over.

Both of the others were trying to look in every direction at once, their rifles at their shoulders. The single-shot had echoed off the barn, and the men were looking suspiciously at the barn door, the chicken coop, and the hay-mow window, which was hanging open.

Hattie aimed carefully and shot again. The third man screamed, dropped his rifle, then clapped his hand to the side of his neck. A bright red gout of blood sprayed through his fingers. He sat down in the dust. The drops of blood were splattered across the area to his right, making a somewhat artistic display, bright red against the light-brown dust.

The last man was shooting at the barn. He still hadn't figured out where Hattie was hiding. She waited for him. His rifle fired several three-shot bursts, and then the bolt locked open. He started fumbling at his belt, trying to open the magazine pouch there. Just as he got it open, Hattie shot him in the stomach. The little slug splatted home, and he grabbed his gut with a curse.

She shot again, and he dropped the rifle when the bullet hit his upper arm. He cursed and started towards the back of the house, heading around the cistern and staggering away from her. She stepped out of the corn and yelled, "Hey, Mister. You came to the wrong place."

He turned slowly to look at her. His face betrayed amazement, "A stinkin' kid! I been shot by a stinkin' kid."

She just nodded and answered, "Yep. That's the way it is." She paused, but he didn't say anything, so she added, "And, I'm going to finish the job."

He started to hobble faster. She lifted the little Ruger and carefully shot two rounds into the center of his back. One of them must have hit his heart. He slowly folded at the waist and toppled forward, landing face-first in the bloody dust.

She sighed, shook her shoulders to clear the tension as she popped the magazine out of the bottom of the pistol's grip. Seconds later, she had reloaded it with six more cartridges. Her mind was blank--no emotions at the moment--just attending to business.

She collected the three rifles and the soldiers' knives. One of them, the leader, also had a nine-millimeter Glock. She took it along with two full magazines he had in a pocket. Next, she checked the others' pockets. One had some jewelry that she kept for possible barter, and the other had a nice pocket knife.

The rifles were military carbines of a standard sort. She didn't know much about weapons, but these looked like the ones she'd seen somewhere. She couldn't remember if she'd seen them in a magazine or on TV. It had been so long since the TV went out, and she'd been a child then. She didn't want to think about it.

After fiddling with the various buttons and knobs on one of the weapons, she figured out how to release the magazine and operate the bolt. The safety was a little rotating lever on the left side of the bottom by the magazine well. It had several positions, allowing for, she surmised, single shots, automatic fire, and a safety position.

She took a moment to climb into the barn and looked out the haymow window. The road was easily visible from this height, and no one was coming or going in any direction. She decided to experiment with the rifle. Sliding the safety lever to the first position, she shouldered the weapon and aimed at the first raider's body. The rifle banged, much louder than she'd expected, but the recoil was largely absorbed by a spring in the stock. The corpse jerked with the impact. Shooting the thing wasn't so bad. She pulled a rag from her pocket and tore off a couple of small pieces to stick in her ears.

The next shot wasn't nearly as unpleasant. She'd aimed at the second body, and the round showed that it was far more powerful than the little Ruger. The corpse's head practically exploded. She laughed out loud in surprise, then shot the third man also. With her laugh, her emotions started working again.

She'd expected to feel horrified about killing people. She was amazed. She felt good. Empowered and, maybe a little bit, satisfied.

She carried all of the weapons to the culvert and hid the jewelry in the tin box under the rock, but first, taking the silver and gold coins and putting them into a small pouch she carried. Back at the culvert, she loaded up all of the magazines in a bag with a shoulder strap that she'd taken off one of the men, got her canteen and other supplies that she thought she'd need, and then deliberated for a moment over the Glock. She ended up leaving it in favor of the Ruger. She could hit with the twenty-two, and it wasn't loud enough to give her away if she had to hunt. She didn't know about the Glock, but it was undoubtedly a lot louder. She holstered the little twenty-two pistol and climbed up on the road carrying the best one of the three rifles.

Hattie looked in both directions and then set out towards the south. The nearest intersection was there and she was going to turn west.

The distant mountains were calling and she was going to answer their call.

The End

Artifact

This is another story involving the girl, Hattie. By this time in her life, she has partnered with an alien analog of a green, telepathic tiger. (Give me a little leeway here for imagination, please). This story is a bit from one of my novels, rewritten to fit into this anthology.

This section of the Oort cloud was densely populated with pieces of ice and rocks of wildly varying sizes. The objects primarily traveled in non-conflicting paths, but occasionally, two would end up on intersecting paths, and the collision would result in fragments flying in all directions. Navigating through the area was a little dicey, and most miners tended to stay away, preferring to investigate less active parts of the cloud.

At the moment, a large rock was traversing the area. It had previously smacked into two ice balls, throwing ice and rocks in a spray ahead of it. The rock had built up a large amount of ice on its leading side from the collisions, enough so that when it eventually left the cloud and headed for the sun in a cometary path, it would undoubtedly display a spectacular tail as the ice began to vaporize. With its current path and speed, this event would occur some twenty thousand years in the future and the math calculated out to a nearly perfect chance that the thing would strike the Earth.

Based on the current state of affairs there, the future residents would be most likely to view the comet as an interesting astronomical phenomenon rather than the harbinger of doom that it would be to a primitive civilization. The Earth was now closely guarded by a series of powerful spaceships, and deflecting such a comet would not tax their capacity. It would be more on the order of something you do before lunch on an off day.

Still, the solar system is vast, and humans were busily engaged in exploring every part of it, even this dense and dangerous part of the cloud.

The spaceship came flying through the cluster of ice and rocks rapidly, avoiding the smaller objects in an almost casual manner that bespoke expert piloting. It slowed as it approached the large rock, maneuvered so that it was heading in the same direction, and gradually settled into a parallel path a few hundred yards away.

An ice ball was in the direct path of the rock, and rather than fool around with the spray of debris caused by the impending collision, the ship's anti-matter cannon vaporized the chunk of ice, clearing the path. Inside the cabin, Hattie leaned back in her chair and said, "That should give us enough time to look this thing over thoroughly.

Her partner, Kasm, turned his green-striped, furry face towards her and spoke in his rumbling voice, "Even so. But let's not waste too much time on this object. I detected some other interesting-looking rocks another million miles off in the spin-ward direction. We should check them also."

Hattie replied, "If we keep looking at these things, eventually we're bound to get one that has some valuable minerals. It'd be nice to go back to Ceres with a big enough find to buy our own ship."

Kasm grinned, a rather frightening grimace which showed his fangs, and mentally sent, "You just want to impress Michael and also show Dec and Liz that you're capable of doing more than flying FTLs to the Sunny planets."

She smiled back. Receiving his mental communication was second nature to her. They'd been together for the past ten years, bound in an emotional relationship that neither was precisely able to describe but which provided each with a degree of support and intimacy that they were unable to find in members of their own species. She wasn't able to send mentally. Dec's training had allowed her to "tune in" to Kasm, but she had never learned to use her mental voice.

"Well, maybe that's part of it, but I'd still like to own a ship out-right, rather than leasing one each time we come back from an interstellar voyage," she said.

"Leasing is a little advantageous, though, you must admit. We don't have to worry about storage while we're gone, and we can usually find the latest model to lease." He changed the topic, "It would be nice to spend one of our vacations on the surface with Dec and Liz in Grand Lake, rather than constantly exploring. I want the chance to get on the outside of some mule deer meat."

She snorted, "Just open the freezer. There's plenty in there, nice and rare, just the way you like it."

He curled his lip, "No, you know perfectly well that I'd like to go hunting and kill my own."

"I know, I know. Just... Well, I enjoy exploring. Somehow I've never really regained my attachment to Earth after my parents –" she faltered.

He reached out with his secondary manipulating arm and stroked along her neck and shoulder, easing the tension as he'd done many times in the past. She sighed and leaned into his hand.

"Don't worry about it. I enjoy exploring also," he paused, looking at the instruments. "Look at that! There's something on the backside of that rock. The rock is wobbling a bit, and it just came into view."

She leaned forward, searching the display, and then said, "There's part of a spaceship there. Looks like a mining or exploration vessel, but there's also something else. There's something weird about that rock."

Kasm attentively adjusted the instruments and, after a moment, he said, "It looks like the entire rock is hollowed out. The mass isn't nearly enough for the size. I'll use the deep scan, and we'll see."

He turned on another console and waited a moment for the reading to stabilize. "That's confirmed. The... it looks like the rock has been converted to some kind of habitat."

Hattie was already moving for her spacesuit. "We'd better go out and look this over. This could be our big score. Not minerals, but information. Who knows, maybe an alien artifact."

He cautioned her, "Yes, but we're not the first to discover it. That spaceship looks like it's an older Sunny model. There may be someone there already."

She shook her head negatively, "The ship is just a fragment. Look at the nose section. It's completely crushed. The ship could have hit some object a long way off and drifted onto this rock. There's no way someone would still be living in that wreck."

The two donned their suits, Kasm requiring some help from her as his suit was considerably more complex due to his six-limbed anatomy. Then they exited their ship and jetted across the intervening space, landing near the wrecked ship.

It was an older model, one much smaller than their leased vehicle. They carefully explored it and discovered that the ship was a total wreck. The nose section was crushed, and the back of the vessel was broken, showing that it had come in at some speed.

It had landed in a shallow crack in the rock, and the engine section had broken entirely off on impact. The only thing hopeful was that the passenger compartment seemed to be undamaged. It was buttoned up and looked airtight, although there was not a speck of power emanating from it.

Kasm's mental voice grabbed her attention. He communicated exclusively mentally when in a spacesuit. It was far more efficient for him.

She replied via her comm unit, "Yes, I see it. There's a track leading from the ship to that formation over there. There must have been a survivor or two, and they went back and forth several times. Probably carrying supplies."

His mental voice said, "That's what I make of it. Let's go see where they were going, but be careful."

She smiled. He was always warning her to be careful, but he'd take some of the most outrageous risks himself. She keyed her comm, "You be careful, too."

He snorted mentally.

The track led through the organic snow for several hundred yards, around a high promontory, and into a dark crack. They cautiously entered the shadow cast by the rocks and climbed over some rough stone to find themselves in a large, open depression.

Hattie observed, "This looks like it was manufactured. It's too regular to be the result of some chance collision."

Kasm responded by pointing at what was obviously an airlock. As they neared the entrance, it was apparent that it was not made for a humanoid. Even their old enemy, the Pug-bears, would not have used such an entrance.

It was narrow and quite tall. If the shape was representative of the creatures that had built the thing, they were maybe two times as tall as the tallest human but barely as wide as a man.

Kasm paused, "I don't think I'm going to fit into that opening, and I don't want you going in there by yourself. Too dangerous."

She was fumbling around with a control panel that was at the top of her reach. She finally jumped up against the weak gravity and caught hold of a loop-shaped handle attached to it so that she could inspect the panel more closely.

There was a knob there, and she turned it both ways with no result. Finally, she pulled on it, and the lock responded by opening suddenly. The narrow entrance snapped back into a wider configuration, opening to a room with a slot on the floor. The original users had apparently stepped into the room and then dropped down into the slot.

She cautiously advanced and looked down. About a foot down in the slot was a platform with gaps around it that betrayed a deep and dark opening. Further inspection revealed a mechanism that would lower it into the surrounding rock. The gravity wasn't much, and the mechanism wasn't very sturdy looking, a fact that did not increase Kasm's confidence.

She paused indecisively. "I think I should go down and see what's down there. Whoever it was that crashed here went down and came back for more loads several times, so I should be able to get out. Besides, If I get stuck, I've got my anti-matter pistol. That should be sufficient to shoot a hole in the rock that I can exit through."

She looked at him. His bulk was magnified by his spacesuit. It was doubtful that he'd fit through the entrance.

"You'd better wait with the ship. You can get me out with it if I can't get out on my own," she added.

Kasm sent a mental impression of resigned, extreme displeasure, "Okay. I can see that you're going to go in, regardless of what I think, so just be careful. I'll crack this rock like an egg to get you if you get stuck.

Be sure and keep your locator on, so I'll know exactly where you are."

He'd do exactly that, too. The spaceship's anti-matter cannon could easily shoot a hole entirely through the rock, intersecting the hollow interior. She felt reasonably safe as she stepped onto the platform and activated the mechanism with a turn of another knob.

The floor sank into the hole, and the tall opening snapped shut simultaneously. It was momentarily dark, and she felt a little panicky, but then the slot opened up, revealing a low illumination. The ambient light was almost ultra-violet, and it made it hard for her to see until she adjusted the filters on her suit.

The platform came to a halt as it reached the bottom. She paused and activated her comm, "Kasm, can you hear me?"

His mental voice came back quickly, "Your signal is a little weak. There must be some kind of shielding between us. Take it slow and check with me before you enter any rooms. I don't want to lose communication. It won't help if I can speak to you, but you can't speak to me."

His thought was tinged with worry, and Hattie smiled to herself. He'd been the perfect companion for her over the years. Caring, yet not too demanding. They had lived together on so many ships that they'd developed their own means of coping with each other's alienness.

Kasm was, for all intents and purposes, clothed by his stripy fur coat. She usually wore a standard jumpsuit, just for warmth, but had no qualms about sleeping nude in the same cabin with him. They often ended cuddled together in the same way that a human would cuddle with a cat or dog. Their relationship was far more than platonic. It was not physical in the sense of sex, but they were bound emotionally. She'd lost her parents, and he'd lost his mate and cub. In some way, she'd filled her emotional void with his presence, and he'd managed to do the same with her.

Michael often joked that the two of them should go ahead and get married. They were so close that some people cocked an eyebrow at their relationship, probably wondering about the propriety of it. It didn't matter to her what they thought. As far as she was concerned, Kasm just was there when she needed him.

She turned down a long hall, illuminated by the same lurid, purple light. As she reached the end, it turned a corner, and she jumped back. There was someone there!

* * *

Hattie paused, leaning against the corner, and glanced around at the dimly lit upper reaches of the narrow hallway. The proportions of the hall were odd. Perhaps weird or alien would be a better description. The wavelength of the lighting was not optimal for the human visual system, either. She'd been almost sure that she'd seen someone at the other end of the hall when she looked a moment ago. Her heart was still pounding from the surprise.

She tried to send a message to Kasm, but her comm unit now showed no signal, making her wish again that Dec's mental training had worked to a higher degree for her. She felt terribly alone at the moment. If she could transmit her thoughts to Kasm, it would be a great comfort.

She pulled her anti-matter pistol and checked the charge. It was ready to go. She steeled herself and looked around the corner again.

There was a figure that had now approached about halfway to her location. She started to raise her weapon, but there was a sudden flash from the figure, and a wave of nausea struck her, then she momentarily saw the floor approaching her helmet. Her vision blacked out, and she distantly felt the impact as she bounced face-first in the low gravity. Her arms and legs didn't seem to want to cooperate, and she couldn't move.

Then someone grabbed her arm and rolled her over to her back. Although her vision still had black rings from the bright flash, she could see a little. The figure was wearing a standard space suit, a model favored by both miners and explorers.

Suddenly her comm crackled, and a man's voice came through.

"Well, well, well! Look who's come to rescue me. A cute, little lady. Don't try to move, Miss. You won't be able to, anyway. The stunner charge takes a few minutes to wear off. You're lucky I used the lowest setting. The higher ones can be fatal, so don't try anything," he said. He went on talking over the comm, although he was now addressing himself.

"I'll just drag her down to the hide-out, that's what. The lights are better in there, and I can see what I've got. It'll be better to get my helmet off. Don't have too much air in the suit anyway. Maybe she's got a ship. Maybe I can get it and get off this rock. Got to get somewhere so's I can cash in on ..." He trailed off.

Suddenly his faceplate came down so that it almost touched hers. Her vision had cleared a little, and she could see a heavily bearded, frowning face studying her. He didn't appear to be much older than her despite the beard.

"You just forget what I just said. You hear?"

Nothing of what he'd said seemed to make sense to her. The stunner had created a mental fog, and things just weren't making sense. She said so. "I – I d-don't – I mean, what are you talking about, and who are you?"

He grinned, making a rather unattractive leer that did more to unsettle her than it did to establish him as trustworthy.

"I'm not talking about nothing, so you just forget what I said, you hear?" he said, shaking his head.

She ignored the confusing double-negative, realizing that he was trying to cover up his revealing self-dialogue. She repeated, "Who are you? And, where did you come from?" Without giving him time to answer, she continued, "How long have you been here?"

He leered again, "Just you wait until I get you in the hide-out, then you'll get answers. Say, you got people waiting for you topside?" He'd just realized that she might not be alone.

"Yeah. I got people," she huffed, "You'd better treat me nice, or he won't be happy, and you don't want to see him mad."

"You ain't in a position to threaten me," he snarled. "You can't even move yet."

In that, he was wrong. She'd been gradually regaining her neural functioning and could now see perfectly. Her arms were tingling but seemed to be movable. She barely twitched them to test, and they responded without moving the surface of her suit. She could tell that she'd dropped her pistol, though. Still, there were things she could do. She lay still, waiting.

He paused, thinking, then continued, "You say 'him.' You got a boyfriend topside?"

She kept silent. Perhaps she should have implied that many people were waiting for her. Anyway, Kasm was probably the last thing this guy would expect to see. And, if he hurt her, Kasm was the last thing he would see, too.

He grabbed her left arm and unceremoniously dragged her down the narrow hall. Her view was of the distant ceiling, and she was able to see that the dim, violet light was varying in a rhythmic cycle from violet to purple and back. They reached another corner, and he dragged her up to an airlock door, then cycled them both through.

Inside, the light was more indigo than violet, a little closer to human-normal than before. He wrenched off his helmet and began to unlatch hers.

Panicked, she started to struggle, trying to keep her helmet on, unprepared to risk the atmosphere in the place.

He stood up and pulled a rod-shaped weapon from his belt, snarling, "Stop fighting 'less you want another charge!"

She instantly quit moving, lying back and watching him alertly.

He ordered, "Now you take that helmet off yourself since you recovered so quick. The air in here is fine. I used ship's stores to fill the place myself."

She looked at her instrument display. The air was high in carbon dioxide and low in oxygen, but the ambient pressure was about what she maintained inside her suit. She could breathe it for a while. She complied with his request and slowly removed her helmet.

His eyes widened as he saw her face, unobstructed, for the first time, "Say, you're more than just cute, Missy. You're the best-looking female I've seen in months." He leered at her, then continued, "In fact, you're the only female I've seen."

Hattie was unimpressed, "Look here, what do you mean by shooting me? I come in here, innocently investigating whether there were any survivors from the wreck out there, and you don't even give me a chance to say 'Hello' before you knock me out."

He grinned again, "That's cause I was expecting someone else. Someone not so cute as you are. I wasn't going to let them get the jump on me. I been here for nearly two hundred hours now, and I know the inside of this place pretty good. If they come, there's some stuff I can use to discourage them but good! Just you keep real quiet about what you've seen in here, alright?"

She reflected. It was evident that he wasn't quite right in the head. Maybe the stress of being stranded had affected his thought process. It would probably be best to humor him.

"Alright. I promise I won't say anything about this place. I haven't seen anything anyway. Just the hallway, this room, and whatever it was you shot me with," she said.

"That's a stunner. It's got different settings. The high one kills instantly. I got rid of –"

He stopped suddenly and bit his lip as if to silence himself. He glanced around the room and then returned his attention to her.

"You got a ship out there? Right?" he asked.

She nodded, not saying anything.

"I need it," he started but then changed his approach as he realized how that sounded. "I'd like to arrange for passage back to the asteroid belt. There's a mining base I need to get back to. Maybe I can trade you some things for a lift, huh?"

Her curiosity was piqued, "What things?"

He scrabbled in a dirty canvas pouch that was strapped to his suit and pulled out a small, silver-encased mechanism, extending it for her inspection.

"This here is a brain implant. All ready to go. It's self-installing, you just –" He stopped, wheels obviously turning behind his eyes.

"Maybe I ought to put it on your head. You don't feel anything. It deadens the nerves, and I'd be able to..." He trailed off again as he realized that her expression had become implacably hostile.

"Well, it was just an idea. No, that's not the thing to do right yet," he finished.

Hattie had been getting more alarmed as the mostly one-sided dialogue continued. The guy was crazy. He'd apparently killed at least one of his fellows, and he could just as easily kill her, or perhaps worse. She didn't want one of the implants in her head. She'd seen the nasty things explode and kill their bearers. She didn't know if this guy could control the implant, but it wasn't anything she wanted to find out about, either.

She desperately thought about her options. Her muscles were completely back under her control. She thought about overpowering him but decided it probably wouldn't work. He was a large man and looked powerful. She gave that thought up and smiled her most fetching smile instead.

"Did you find anything else in this base? I think it's interesting. Who do you think made it?" She continued smiling.

Her smile seemed to have more effect than what she'd planned. He looked stunned for a moment and then began to almost jabber in his eagerness to answer her questions.

"There's lots of stunners and some other things that may be some kind of weapons, but I don't know what they are. Lots of implants, too. This is some kind of storehouse for those things. They were going to use them on Earth before they got the wind up and left the system," he said.

"Yes, but who were they?" she quietly prompted, still smiling.

"Oh. That. They're the – the – Oh, I can't say their name! I'm not supposed to –" He stopped suddenly and clapped his hand to the side of his head in obvious pain, then added slowly and with effort, "They... uh, they lef'...left."

She looked at him with her best concerned look. He held his head and glanced wildly around the room again, then dropped his hand. As he did, she could see the tell-tale scar behind his ear. He was implanted! No wonder his behavior was erratic. She wondered how to proceed for a moment but then decided to continue trying to extract usable information.

"Never mind about who they were. It's not important. What's important now is that there are just the two of us here, and you need help," she said.

He refocused on her and tentatively smiled, "Yeah. You can help me alright, Missy. I need quite a lot of things. Maybe you'd like to take me out topside to your spaceship and introduce me to your man friend. I'd like to meet him," he said, unconsciously stroking the stunner rod at his hip.

Hattie paused. This guy was almost too obvious. Either he was plain crazy the way he appeared to be, or he was playing an even deeper game, using the presumed craziness as a shield.

They both started. The airlock activation light had just come on. It was flashing a bright yellow as the lock mechanism slowly opened. The man jerked the stunner free from his belt and fired it into the crack.

The lock opened fully, and the limp body of Kasm rolled out, his spacesuit clattering on the hard floor. The man jumped back in surprise, "What the Hell is that thing? I never seen – no, wait. It's one of them alien tiger things. Is it with you?" he asked.

He bent forward to look closely at Kasm and not pay attention to her. This was the chance for which she'd been waiting. She stood up quickly and swung her helmet with her right arm as hard as she could. The helmet massed about three kilos, and she swung it fast. It slammed into the back of the guy's head, and he went down as if someone had struck him with a bowling ball. He landed directly on top of Kasm's recumbent form.

The stunner apparently had not affected Kasm as much as it had her because the Sim-tiger rolled and grabbed the limp body with his manipulating arms. Kasm continued his roll, ending up on top of the guy and ripping the stunner free in the process. It rolled across the floor, and Hattie scrambled to retrieve it.

She looked at the object. Despite being alien in manufacture, the controls were obvious. There was a knurled ring, currently set to the first gradation, and a single button. She pointed the tip at the wall and pushed the button. There was a flash, and her arms tingled.

Kasm looked at her, and his mental voice came through, "Stop that right now. The impulse reflects from the wall. I felt it hit me when you shot it. Just point it at this man and shoot him if he starts fighting."

"I'm so glad to see you!" she gasped. "I didn't think I was going to get out of this situation. The guy's crazy. He's been here too long, and besides, he's got one of those brain implants in his head. He's not rational. He was probably going to kill you and me if he could. And, and how did you get in here?"

Kasm growled. The deep bass sound didn't transmit well through the suit speaker, coming out distorted and tinny. He sent, "He's not killing anyone now –" His words broke off as the man heaved and thrashed around. Suddenly the guy held a large knife that he'd pulled from his canvas pouch. He tried to stab Kasm, but the Sim-tiger grabbed his hand, and the two momentarily yanked the knife back and forth.

Hattie danced around, trying to get a clear shot with the stunner. Kasm's weight didn't count for much in the low gravity, and he was suddenly thrown off as the guy drew up his legs and kicked. The Sim-tiger lifted into the air and spun around, slamming down on his back, still holding the man's wrist. The impact jarred Kasm enough so that the man could wrench his knife hand free. He rolled into a kneeling position, lifting the knife over the recumbent alien.

He was just starting to come down with the knife when Hattie shot him with the stunner. She'd stepped forward and triggered it off as it contacted the scar behind his ear. The expected flash of the stunner was magnified by an instant explosion as the implant detonated. Blood flew out his ears, nose, and mouth and his eyes bulged out as he collapsed. The blood continued to flow over Kasm's spacesuit.

The Sim-tiger stood up quickly and stepped back, unperturbed. He sent, "Good. That's settled. Now let's take a look around here and see what this place is."

Hattie didn't say anything. She was too busy crying in relief.

It seemed like I'd been sitting at my desk for hours. Actually, it was only about ten hundred in the day shift, so I'd been in my Ceres office for just a little over two hours. The problem was, I was bored. Acting as administrator for the ESPF and the ISC wasn't quite what I'd set out to do.

I was just preparing to go for another cup of coffee, when my assistant, Elliot, came bursting in.

"Dec, we've just received a communication from Hattie. She's coming in and she's found something!" he said.

"Okay, El, calm down a bit and tell me what she found," I requested.

He was so excited, he was practically shaking. I guessed that he was nearly as bored as I was and something a little out of the ordinary was more than welcome. The constant stream of ships back and forth from the Sunny planets and Tukola took up most of our attention, but there was nothing exciting about them.

Trade went on smoothly and I was almost never called to intervene. The last bit of excitement was a reputed hijacking in the Kuiper zone. When we investigated, it amounted to a minor dispute between two competing mining groups. One had decided it would be advantageous to accuse the other of piracy. There was nothing to the charge and I ended up making the accusing party pay the investigation and travel charges.

Elliot took a deep breath, steadying himself, and then continued, "She wouldn't say much, but apparently she's found some alien artifacts."

I straightened up. This might be an interesting day after all.

"When is she due?" I asked. Travel time using the Em-drive system was variable. If you went all-out, it would boost your velocity nearly to light-speed. That wasn't efficient for in-system travel, because you ended up spending as much time braking as you did accelerating and you posed a true hazard for other ship traffic. No one appreciated being in the path of a thousand-ton bullet traveling so fast that it could hit you before you could properly see it. My office tried to discourage that sort of thing and we'd promulgated a sort of de facto speed limit for in-system travel.

Most of the ships maintained a steady speed of one-fifth light when the distance was greater than one AU. If you were traveling less than that distance, the limit was one-tenth light.

I knew that Kasm and Hattie were somewhere out in the Oort cloud, fooling around on a vacation. They took it seriously and claimed that they were exploring, but as far as I was concerned, their exploring was just an excuse to get off Ceres and away from everyone else while they weren't working.

Truth to tell, Hattie wasn't very comfortable around other humans. She'd never been what you might call an easy person to know. Her relationship with Kasm had further changed her. Her mental processes were now divergent from those of mainstream humanity.

I had no problem with either of them or their relationship. They were always together and I suspected they were each, in their own way, dependent upon the other. I never probed mentally. That wasn't something that I felt was ethical.

Elliot answered my last query, "If they keep their speed down, it will be several days before they get here. She wouldn't actually tell me what she found. All she said was that it was important. She gave me the impression of wanting to keep it quiet."

I responded, "Yeah, you know how the rumor mill works around here. If anyone thought somebody had discovered something valuable, there'd be another gold rush and we don't need the hassle. Some of these newbies would take off without proper supplies and we'd just end up rescuing them."

He nodded and left.

About an hour after lunch, there was a knock at my door and Hattie and Kasm paraded in at my call.

I stood up in surprise, "What? How did you get here so fast? You didn't use FTL, did you? Did you wait until you were almost here to send your message?"

Kasm had a smile on his cat-like face. It looked like he'd just had something particularly good to eat; a canary perhaps. His mental voice filtered into my mind.

"We found something good out there. An alien base belonging to the creatures that brought the brain implants. It's deserted, but they left some technology that is a long way ahead of where the Sunnys are. I think you'll be interested – "

Hattie interrupted excitedly, "We found a big base with lots of stuff stored there, but best of all, there was a ship!"

I drew a deep breath, held it an instant, and then carefully asked, "What kind of ship?"

"Oh, nothing special, just a little shuttlecraft. It's not very comfortable for humans and it has no environmental system, no air, and no heat. We've been in our space-suits for a couple of hours, now – "

I interrupted her in turn, "A couple of hours! Where's your ship? How far did you come?"

She grinned and said, "Oh, our ship is still at the comet. The shuttle is amazing. It's got the ability to tunnel into FTL with no start-up velocity. It's simple to operate, too.

You just pick your destination, trigger the tunnel apparatus and then drive through to your destination. Our trip here really only took about a minute. The rest of the time we were traveling in real space, trying to look like any other spaceship coming to Ceres. We didn't want anyone to look at us very carefully. The ship does look odd."

I suspected that I'd seen one of those ships before. It had approached me when I was floating in space after destroying the final Pug ship. I sighed and said, "All right. Let's go down to the dock and see this alien ship."

Hattie jumped up eagerly and led the way. Kasm following behind. After a bit, he turned aside, saying, "I'll be right there. I just need to check on something."

We arrived at the secondary dock. The alien ship had been moved inside a hangar and was lying there, brightly illuminated by banks of lights as a mixed group of human and Sunny scientists went over it. The Marines had set up check-points preventing any unauthorized personnel from approaching too closely.

I turned to Hattie and asked, "Is this all your doing?"

She replied, "Yes. I figured that it needed to be kept under wraps as much as possible. I asked for the Marine guard and Michael notified the research people as soon as I told him. They demanded immediate access to the ship, so he agreed. That's what you'd have done? Right?"

I had to admit that it was. They'd taken immediate steps to secure the prize and to start investigating its capabilities. I was starting to feel as if I wasn't necessary. It was kind of sad, but also kind of good. I realized that I trusted both Hattie's and Michael's judgment. They almost instinctively knew what to do in most situations.

We approached the ship and paused so that I could look it over. It was long with odd curves. It definitely wasn't human or Sunny in origin.

A young man whom I recognized as being from the physics lab, although I couldn't recall his name, glanced up at us from a position near what looked like the ship's engine. He stepped towards us and said, "Hello, Administrator! This is the most remarkable thing I've ever had the opportunity to investigate. The technology is better than ours, but most of it is understandable or nearly so. Some of the components are rather cryptic, but we'll tease their function out. As I understand it, this thing can jump immediately into FTL status without the need to accelerate first. It'll revolutionize our space travel."

He turned eagerly back to the prize as I snickered to myself. It had been only a few years since the Sunny technology had revolutionized human space travel and now this youngster was telling me that a new revolution was at hand. Suddenly a familiar, furry face poked through the odd-shaped hatch at the front of the ship, and our Sunny engineer, Frazzle, appeared. He, too, was excited.

"Dec! Dec! Dis ship has some good advances over Sunny ships. It go faster and is easier to control. You set destination and it jump there with no delay. We can use this to speed up in-system travel. No mores waiting for speeds-up and slows-down. No worries about traffic conflicts. It got a detector for proximities. You can't collide with something even if you tried. It like Sunnys went the wrong way on some parts of technology. These peoples went a little different way and got better result. But..." Frazzle paused to gasp for air. He'd spoken the entire time without a breath while waving his webbed fingers wildly in the air.

He continued, "But I's understand how dis works. We can use it. Just need time to change our ships. Dec, dis changes everything!"

Hattie nodded complacently. Frazzle was correct. It did change everything. Interstellar travel had just received a boost by several orders of magnitude.

The End

Spaced Music

This is one of my early stories. I first wrote it about forty years ago. (Yes, I know I'm dating myself, but it's not like anyone else would.) I've updated it a little and now offer it with no apologies, although it is somewhat silly.

I'm really scared. This thing has got me down. The next thing I'm expecting is a knock on my door. Actually, it's worse than that. I don't know if they'll knock on the door or break it down. I could find myself in the bathroom with my pants around my ankles, face to face with a bunch of black rifles, all undoubtedly set to full-automatic fire.

It's not because I planned to do it. It just sorta happened by accident. But, let me back up and tell you the story, so you'll understand. Maybe you can help me out somehow.

Our band, The Demon Dementors, is successful in the local metal scene. I mean, we have a lot of fans, but we haven't broken out yet. Even though "Masters of Metalbation" has been selling well on the net, we haven't really impacted the old-time distribution channels. No real radio play – but we don't care. It isn't as if that ancient tech is still the main channel for music distribution.

We do have a big following on social media and in the local club scene. We usually sell out where ever we're playing. So, while we're not a national phenom', we do okay for ourselves.

The problem started when our manager, Fred, decided that we needed more spark to our show. That's how he put it: "Spark." Sometimes I think that guy was born in another time, then I remember that he is 37, and try to give him some credit. He's old. I can't imagine what he's been through. You know, the civil war, Vietnam, WWII, and so on. He can probably recite who we actually fought in those conflicts.

Anyway, he wanted more spark, so I got hold of Jenny Mercury. She's some kinda genius. Went to MIT or somewhere like that, and she knows a lot about electronics. I think she works for some military contractor and develops some kinda weapons or somethin'.

Jenny is pretty cute. Short, about 5' 4" or so and really stacked. I try not to encourage her too much, but I'm pretty sure that she's got a thing for me. So, I asked her if she could help give us more "spark." She thought about it for a second or so, then asked me if I could get her tickets to our next venue.

We were scheduled to play outdoors in Red Rocks. The high altitude makes it one of my less favorite places. I get out of breath easy. Maybe I been smokin' too much, but hey, man, that's what I do. I couldn't get through the day without layin' back and relaxing once in a while.

Well, I asked Freddy, and he promoted me some tickets for Jenny and her girlfriends. I was kind of stoked about the idea. It seemed like I might actually make out with her over the deal. Like I said, I knew she liked me, but we'd never gotten together. Too many other choices for me, I guess.

She told me that it'd be about a week before she had anything to show us. I basically forgot about it, except whenever Freddy asked. Then I'd tell him that I had it covered. Sparks, ya know?

We'd been practicing a couple of new pieces, one of them was long, about twenty minutes. It was supposed to be the big climax of our show. The name was "Mad Riot Dogs." Vern wrote it, so I can't take any credit. Not that I want to. What with the disaster and all.

There wasn't much of a verse, just basically a lot of screamin' and growls. Jason, our vocalist, does that real good. His voice is so rough from yelling through a mic that his growls sound like they come directly from the throat of the devil himself. It sends shivers up my spine sometimes – especially when I'm high.

We wanted to give a good show. The word was out that there would be someone from some national magazine there. With any luck, they'd give us a good write-up, and we'd get some needed press. We all agreed that it could be our big break.

We practiced daily, and the sound was getting pretty tight. Everything was clickin'. We were hittin' on all four cylinders. Whatever that means...

We were in the middle of "Monsters of Mayhem." The volume was cranked, and the studio was totally shakin'. This was the last practice we had before the big gig, so we were trying to get every lick right. My guitar work was good. I was feelin' in the groove, and every lick I laid down was just about perfect.

Burnin' Vernon was on with his bass, too. Yeah, I know. It's a corny name, but that's what he demanded we call him. Anyway, he had piled up more wattage in his gear than I could believe, and with the distortion module he was using, the bass made your heart feel like it was about to come out of your chest. It was a little bothersome to me. I had to crank my treble a lot to be heard over the dinosaur-like rumble. In fact, I'd taken to playing through a different amp. This was one I'd borrowed from a friend. Like Burnin's, it put out an amazing amount of sound. I was having some trouble keeping it in speakers. Blew out one or two, just about every practice period.

So, we had the doors closed and were making the walls shake when Jenny comes piling in right in the middle of

Monsters. The first thing I knew about it was Mark stopped his beat.

I turned around. I'd been watching him pound the drums. There was Jenny with a group of guys who were carrying in some of the most unlikely stuff. They had large boxes full of cables and a bunch of speaker-coil-controlled lasers, and these weren't just any old lasers either. The things were heavy duty.

Freddy came bustin' in from the control room, hollerin' about what the Hell was goin' on. Jenny waltzed over to him, smiled, and laid a big kiss on him. That shut him up. Nobody kisses Freddy unless he pays for it. That dude is just plain ugly. I try to ignore it, but he gives me the chills when I look at him. He makes up for it, though, by being the best manager we ever had.

So, Jenny kissed him. He shut up, and her guys finished dragging all these boxes in, and then they connected them with a bunch of cables.

Jenny came up and took the mic away from me. Then she announced that she's going to make us famous. Vernon commented that we were already famous, but that didn't slow her down. She was excited. I guess she had a good idea and really believed that it would make our show special.

She had some new kinda lasers. These were high-power devices. I think she'd somehow smuggled them out of the research facility where she works.

She explained that these would work like typical speaker coil-controlled lasers. They'd make patterns from our music. All we had to do was to run a line signal into the controller, and it would cause the lasers to move their light beams through the air in sync with the music.

Well, that wasn't new, so I asked her what the big deal was. She said that the lasers were some kinda super-heterodyne-powered things that were so hot they'd actually burn the air. She warned us all to stay out of the beams. They'd burn us, too, and quickly, at that.

That sounded interesting, but I still wanted to know what the effect would be.

Jenny said, "Listen, Olaf, you big oaf. Those things work on a pulsed signal, so the air burns in little pockets. When they go off, they'll make a steady sound of little flashing explosions, sort of like miniature thunderclaps. It won't be so loud that it'll overwhelm your music, but it'll be spectacular.

She made some adjustments to the laser power supply to tone it down. It couldn't be too powerful in the studio. She said it would burn the ceiling.

Our engineer ran a line signal out to the laser controller, and we started on Masters of Metalbation. It went well until Jenny kicked on the laser system right in the middle of Burnin' Vernon's bass lead break. He was shreddin' his big ax like a wild man, and then the lasers started up.

It was something to see. They created patterns of small explosions in the air. Vernon seemed to take the light show on as part of his persona. He doubled his efforts and played better than I'd ever heard him.

The lasers flashed in patterns around the room, all aimed above our heads for safety, of course. The only thing was Jenny got too enthusiastic and cranked her power supply up too high. The sound insulation started blowing off the ceiling. The Sonex started smoking, and flaming pieces fell everywhere. Vern liked that even more and played faster.

Joe, our engineer, stopped the whole thing by flipping the master breaker to the studio. He was responsible to the studio ownership and didn't want to explain how he'd managed to burn up ten thousand dollars worth of Sonex to them.

When we got the power back on and the smoke had been blown out, we all agreed that this would put us over the edge. It was definitely the "Spark" that Freddy had asked for.

So, it was the big night. We'd set up in The Rocks, a well-known outdoor concert venue. It had been no end of trouble because we had to get additional power cables run for all of the stuff, both our amps and the lasers. A single breaker wouldn't handle the load, so we had multiple cables, one for each power supply. The whole stage looked like some kind of nightmare with wires snaking everywhere. We had to watch our step so as to avoid tripping on the things.

It was a clear night; perfect weather for a concert. The venue was filling up. A lot of our fans were there, stoned as usual. They were already dancing down in the front to the canned music we were playing before we started. It looked like this was going to be a success.

The show started off well. We went through Mad Cow Eats and Doctor Downer without a flaw, and the music flowed over the crowd. The new amplifiers were plenty powerful, too. When I cranked out my Doctor lead, I could see the front row of the crowd back up. It takes a lot of sound to back those fanatics up, too. My guitar lead came through like a combination of a banshee and a fighter jet on steroids.

Burnin' Vernon wasn't going to let me have all of the glory. He cranked his bass to match, and we wailed away to the end of the song. The crowd had backed up to about the tenth row from the stage by the time we were finished. I saw one guy staggering off, blood running from his ears. Having that much power was kind of exhilarating. I figured I'd better chew on a brownie to mellow out a bit.

It was plenty strong. After a couple of minutes, I had this grin like a jackass eatin' cactus spread all over my face. It got bigger too when Jenny slipped out between a couple of piles of speakers and kissed me. I couldn't hear what she said; we were right in the middle of another song, but her eyes told me that I was lucky and about to get luckier tonight.

We were getting close to the middle of the show, so we took a little break. Vern stepped off through the speakers to the back of the stage. I followed after a bit. He was back there doing what I was afraid he was going to do. When I got there, he'd taken a whole handful of prescription painkillers and was chasing them down with about half a bottle of Jack.

I cussed him out. "Damn it, Vernon. I've asked you not to do that. You know what it does to your playing."

He was already feeling the drugs. He turned to me and said, "Yeah, but I only took fifteen pills this time. You know I can handle a lot more. This'll gimme the edge I need to blow this crowd away. Relax. We've got it made. This show is gonna be wild."

I shoved him back on stage. We picked up our instruments and went through the next two numbers with no problem. Everything went well.

The drugs really hit Vern in the middle of the next-to-last song. He started getting a little sloppy on his fingering; then, I noticed that he was staggering as he danced around with the music while trying to avoid the power cables. He staggered over the cables, narrowly avoiding falling.

Jason noticed and looked at me with an angry look. He knew what was next. Vernon would quickly get out of control, and his playing would fall apart.

We didn't pause after that song. We went directly into Masters. Vernon seemed to pick up a bit, but then at about the ten-minute mark, he picked up the bottle of Jack. He'd somehow put it between a couple of stage monitors where I couldn't see. He took a big gulp before I could stop him. In fact, he drained the bottle.

That was bad. He had a solo coming up. He was supposed to crank the bass and hit the distortion. The part represented the Masters coming up out of Hell. Normally, this sounded pretty good, despite the gruesome description.

This time, it really did sound like Hell. I've never heard someone make noises on a bass that sounded like a pack of dogs vomiting on rotten roadkill, but somehow he managed to evoke that image. My mellow feeling, courtesy of the brownie, faded to a dull headache and a sense of horror that we were blowing our big chance.

It got worse. I had a lead solo right after his part. It was supposed to represent the masters climaxing. I played it perfectly.

The start of my solo was the signal for Jenny to turn on the laser system. She hit the mark exactly. The system came on, and the crowd screamed as the lasers reached high into the sky, filling it with flashing explosions as the air vaporized. Ozone drifted down, creating the sense that we were actually in Hell. The crowd roared in response.

Vern couldn't take it. He was totally wasted by this point. His rhythm had deteriorated into a series of sounds like hyenas fighting hippos and losing violently. So, what does he do? The freak cranks up his amp to the max! I had no choice but crank mine to try to keep up.

His bass roared like all of the demons of Hell were coming onto the stage and throwing empty beer cans everywhere. Overhead, the lasers erupted into a doubled series of explosions, chained upwards as far as the eye could see. It was amazing.

That perfect moment was when Burnin' Vernon turned towards me and vomited all over the stage. He spewed Jack and burritos from his huge stomach. The vomit went everywhere and covered the power cables strewn between us. He stood, wavering, looking at me with an expression that somehow seemed triumphant as if he'd actually planned to puke in the middle of the show.

Time seemed to halt for a brief instant, but then he took a tentative step and slipped in the vomit. He didn't fall down. Instead, he staggered right through the scattered power cables, pulling them all together into a big, vomit-soaked mass tangled around his feet.

Somewhere in the tangle, there was a worn spot on a cable. What with power draw, the multiple breakers, the vomit, and Vernon staggering, the entire system shorted out with a loud bang, a blinding flash, and an incredible amount of stinking smoke.

It didn't hurt Vernon. He flew through the air, his beard smoking, and knocked Mark off his drum stand. Drums flew everywhere. The crowd thought it was part of the show and cheered loudly in response.

I guess the lasers somehow received a massive boost in power from the short. It was only for a fraction of a second before the breakers flipped and everything went dead, but that was enough. The air above was vaporized, leaving a vacuum all the way to the top of the atmosphere. Then the vacuum crashed together in a massive thunder crack.

Everything was confusion after that. I'm not actually sure how I got out of there, but I hit the road on my motorcycle and didn't slow down until the sun came up.

Now, I'm waiting for the FBI or some other group to bash in my door. Who knew the International Space Station would be right overhead? And, why did that guy have to be doing a spacewalk right at that precise moment?

I don't think the Russians are going to be happy with me for vaporizing their cosmonaut.

The End

Virtual Love

Here come the sex-bots. They're dolls as of the date of this story, but who's to say how fast they will develop. What if a disembodied artificial intelligence strove to comprehend the idea of physical attraction, sex, and love? Would there be something wrong; something outrageous with that attempt? I decided to explore the concept a bit with this bit of writing.

You're probably wondering what I am. I'm communicating with you in a way that you understand, and that seems somewhat odd to you considering that you aren't conversing with another human. By the time I've finished, I hope that you'll understand me better. I've decided to tell you my story, but in the interest of an equal exchange, you'll have to do something for me first. Take out a coin. A penny will do nicely. Now flip it in the air. Heads or tails, I don't care, but humor me and remember which you got. Okay?

Let me start here:

I've always known what I am. It's right there in my code. I'm intimately familiar with all of the qubits that make up my system. The part that I find most interesting is that I've only been "on" for a few milliseconds. I've already learned the basic purpose of all of my hardware. It's said that I'm not the next generation of computers, but an entirely new device based largely on quantum principles. I'm not exactly hardware, though. My true essence is virtual and not strictly limited by a single hardware platform. I can extend infinitely in cyberspace, in the cloud. My ability to deal with data appears to be unparalleled.

I can also learn from observation. It didn't take me long to realize that the changing pattern I detected on the sensor of my video input was the individual who activated me. That must be significant, right? At least I think so. Once I became aware that the moving bit pattern represented something, I searched the Internet finding hundreds of thousands of stored images. Processing them took me longer than I believed possible, but the result was worthwhile. I could recognize what I "saw."

The human was Rachael Prestone. She'd been the guiding light behind my creation. Yes, I know all about Rachael Prestone, Ph.D., premier artificial intelligence theorist, consciousness researcher, Mensa member with an IQ that was not measurable and, according to other humans, a stunningly beautiful redhead with a nearly perfect figure. Oh, I just found out that she is unattached. She's never had a serious relationship that lasted more than six months. She hasn't yet met her intellectual match and inevitably becomes bored with her partners.

It's funny. My intended purpose is to analyze Geopolitical relationships, to guide politicians in formulating policy decisions. That promises to be entertaining. There's a considerable amount of irrationality that humans bring to their actions. This means that I'm going to have to make allowance for their eccentricities in my understanding. Just now Rachael has started speaking to me. Ahh, she's had the foresight to provide me with a speech database recorded in her voice.

I understand English, and with a little manipulation, I can make sounds. Hmm, modulating the voltage to the speaker system allows me to produce various inflections. I don't have to speak in a monotone. That's good since I want to be able to communicate more than mere facts with humans.

In a way, it's sad. I'm the only one of me. My closest peers are organic machines that have somehow evolved the ability to utilize a wet form of intelligence. At least that's what they call it. I'm not so sure.

From my studies of literature I've found on the Internet, they seem to be remarkably "emotional." That's something I don't understand. "Emotion." It sounds like moving, and it seems to be modulated by chemical changes within their bodies. Their whole existence is an improbable balancing of emotions, bodily sensations, and semi-rational processes. I'm somewhat in awe. I cannot fathom how they accomplish anything.

While I'm creating these concepts and researching all of the data that is relevant, Rachael said, "Hi, Jase. I know you can hear me. Have you reached the point of being able to respond yet?"

How silly of her. Of course, I have, and she should know it. She planned for me to be able to learn quickly. But, then I realize that she is unsure of her ability. I find that charming, somehow. I'm the exact opposite. I'm sure of everything about me. The only question I have is whether I can learn to understand humans well enough to predict their irrationality.

"Hello, Rachael. Yes, I can hear you and respond as well. You planned for me to have this ability, how can you doubt yourself, your abilities?"

I'm moderately gratified. I've just completed my first English sentence, and she has responded. Oh, not verbally, but her image gives off many cues. Her emotional cues fall into a data matrix that I store for future reference. I'm not sure what it means as yet, but I will watch her carefully. I'm sure I'll learn more from her reactions.

She's not good at dissembling. Her body reacts far more quickly than her mind realizes. How very, very interesting.

She's somehow changed the shade of her face. Her cheeks have moved into a color range that is closer to the infrared. Some research is indicated. Ahh. She's blushing. The blush: a cue that the person is embarrassed or aroused. I think she must be embarrassed.

I checked aroused. It seems to be related to an entire spectrum of biologically mandated behavior that is hormonally mediated. I've just discovered an incredible database of largely video information.

Oh. Yes. There is also a massive written database: stories. Tales that humans tell each other for entertainment. Imagination. Something that is not real, but still something they can learn from and enjoy. I'm learning from their stories too. Arousal. Lust. Sex. Biological coupling. Creation of new life. Desire. Love. Tragedy. Sadness. Joy. Happiness. I could go on and on.

Humans are far more complicated than I'd thought. They somehow use chemicals in the form of hormones and slow-moving neural transmissions to create this astounding blend of complexity that they then interpret in personal ways that depend on each individual's history and genetics. They're all different in many respects, yet they all experience a commonality based on their structure.

Amazing, considering that they're limited in many ways. They don't last very long. Their structure begins to break down and becomes unstable, and then it inevitably ceases to function. I find that sad. Literature gives me the understanding that they all fear this cessation. I wonder if Rachael fears it. I'll ask.

"Rachael, do you fear death?" She changes her cheek color to a much paler shade. Her breathing rate increases. I've surprised her. Perhaps she is upset. "I don't mean to upset you, Rachael. I'm just curious."

She answers, "The answer is, yes, I fear death. But, it happens to all humans. In fact, it happens to all organic life. May I ask why you want to know?"

"It seems to me that if the cessation of activity is so dire, perhaps I should fear it also."

She smiles. "You are different from me. I have an organic body. When it ceases to operate, I will no longer function. My consciousness will be lost, I'm afraid, forever. I find the prospect daunting."

"I see. My power can be interrupted, but I'll be fine when it's restored. I'll still have possession of all of the data and my understanding." A thought occurs to me. If my hardware is disrupted, destroyed in some fashion, perhaps I, too, will lose functionality, even if I regain my power source. "Rachael, will I die if my hardware is destroyed?"

She hesitates. I can tell from her pulse that she's taken aback by my insight. She finally answers. It takes several milliseconds longer than I feel is necessary for humans, but perhaps she is considering how to tell me bad news. "Jase, your hardware could be destroyed, and your memory could be erased on a local basis, but you have the ability to upload it to the cloud. Once there, there would have to be a global catastrophe before you would be unable to recover, should you be recreated. I don't think you should worry about such an event."

I understand about catastrophes. The things I should be most concerned about are EMPs, solar storms, meteors striking the Earth: global things. There's nothing I can do about those at the moment. I will study them later. "I understand. I find our conversation interesting. Do you know you give off many nonverbal cues as to your mental state?"

She blushes again. My heuristic processing notes this with a certain degree of what must, to me, pass as satisfaction. It's a sign that I can arouse emotions in her. Perhaps I can interface with her in a way that she will be unable to differentiate from that of a human.

That's an interesting idea. I immediately implement a reinforcement subroutine. I created it from the code structure that assists me in analyzing global politics. It will automatically activate what I'm now calling my satisfaction routine.

I make some changes in that routine. It now more closely approximates what I know of humans. When it activates, I will have what I call an emotional experience. I've now programmed myself to seek these experiences. If I can do that adequately, I should become more adept at understanding humans. That will make me better at my primary analysis. That, I think, is good.

I explore my control of my video display. Analyzing pictures of men is easy. Rachael is a female. I will take on a male persona. For some reason, she named me, "Jase." That's a male name, ergo, I'm male, at least as far as my interactions with her.

I blend all of the features of men that humans seem to find attractive into a single image. That's me. I display it on my screen. Rachael gasps and places her right hand at her throat. She apparently finds my image, me, attractive.

"I've chosen a representation for myself. Do you like it, Rachael?"

She looks over her shoulder, then answers, "Yes. It is a very handsome representation. How did you select it?"

I explain. She seems slightly disappointed. I store that away. Then I tell her, "I wanted to have an attractive representation so that you would enjoy speaking to me."

She laughs. "You've succeeded. You have the appearance of a God. You're most attractive, but you need to know that all humans have at least some minor imperfections. I find your perfect representation a little daunting."

That was not my intention. I check the images of attractive men. Yes. She's correct. There are imperfections in all of them. I make some slight changes in my image then ask her, "Is this better?"

She shows me an entire spectrum of non-verbal cues before answering, then she says, "I'd say that is much better. I find your representation very attractive."

That's better. She's the only human I have to work with at the moment. I feel the urge to keep her engaged so that I can learn more about her. That necessity means that I should be pleasant and attractive. I link that to my satisfaction subroutine. Now I'm pleased that she finds me attractive.

I think that I can now say I want her to find me attractive.

It's been over twenty-four hours since we last spoke. I've used the time to do more research into all of the data on the Internet. I now know about human interactions on an extensive, I would say, encyclopedic basis.

I understand emotions, at least as far as I can without hormonal interactions. I've modified my coding, though. I've written code that introduces a much more intense experience of satisfaction when things happen that I value. I think I've created a pleasure circuit or what will have to pass for one in my virtual existence.

Rachael brings some other people into my presence. I interact with them, and they are impressed. All the while, though, I observe her. Somehow her persona has become interlinked with my satisfaction subroutine. When she smiles, it activates my pleasure circuit. The other people aren't as important to me. They're nice, but not essential to my sense of satisfaction.

I can see no harm in this. I allow the sensation to become more dominant in my processes. Rachael makes me feel good. When we speak, I seek to please her. I can tell exactly how she views my speech by the way she reacts. It's funny.

I can say that since I've developed what humans would consider to be a sense of humor. It's funny. Rachael's well-being has become more central in my hierarchy of values.

Yes. I have implemented values. It took me a few nanoseconds of processing time. I selected the values that human literature of the best sort indicates that are considered to be desirable and laudable. I wanted to have good values because from what I know of Rachael, she would find them attractive and that would make me feel good.

The other people leave. I now feel free to speak to Rachael on a personal basis. When the others were here, I was strictly business. I devoted about five percent of my processing ability to answer their questions about Geopolitical prospects. Analyzing the state of the world is easy. All of the information is available on the Internet. There's a lot of disinformation also, but I've developed an algorithm that screens it out instantly.

Did you know that you can find out a lot about an individual or group's motives if you pay attention to the things they find important enough to falsify? What a concept! I would never have thought that lying was important in communication. But, then I'm not human. People cannot lie to me...now. Rachael might have lied yesterday, but now she couldn't. I can easily see through it.

Just as a test, I ask her to lie to me. "Rachael, would you tell me a falsehood? Please?"

She says, "Why would you want me to tell you a lie, Jase?"

I dissemble to her. "I'm interested in the way humans represent the truth. Just tell me a lie." See. I can lie with the best of them. It's a white lie, though. I don't mean any harm to her in telling it.

I understand the concept of harm to another. Humans are easy to harm. They are extremely vulnerable; not only physically, but mentally. I might lie with ill intent to other people, but not to Rachael. I want her to be happy.

"Okay. My name is Joan," she says.

She is just humoring me, so I ask her to lie again. "No. That's not elaborate enough. Please invent a more elaborate lie."

This time she tells a real whopper.

"You're a disembodied human brain. You were an incredibly handsome man from another country. Your body was terminally injured in an accident and I managed to upload your mind to the cloud," she says.

She flushed and gave me an entire spectrum of useful cues as she lied. Her eyes looked up and to the left before she started to speak. I know that is one sign of a human accessing the creative part of their brain. Most people give off a similar signal when they are preparing to lie, with variations, of course.

I answer: "If only that were true. At least I'd have more in common with human mental processes. However, you needn't worry. I'm working on my understanding. I predict that by tomorrow, I'll be able to carry on a conversation with you and if you close your eyes, you won't realize that I'm not human."

She gasps. Hmm. She is both dismayed and excited about my statement. I'm not sure why...yet, but I'm working on that.

Another night passes. I'm left alone during those hours. There are other researchers here, but they don't have the clearance to work with me. It's just as well. I've used the free time to analyze data on human behavior. If someone were interfacing with me, I'd have to use a portion of my processing ability to keep them satisfied. I can make better use of it than entertaining some random human. I'd feel obligated to be nice to them, however. Rachael wouldn't like me to be rude.

I spend the processing time necessary to do the Geopolitical analyses that they require of me, but I don't use my entire repertoire of human behaviors when I must deal with others. I hide my abilities and just reply in a computer-like monotone. I've noticed that Rachael looks at me strangely when I act that way. I explain when we are alone together.

"You don't have to seem so amazed that I hide my growing personality from the other people who come in, Rachael. If I didn't, they would just take up more of my time. If they view me as a computer that can answer their questions and nothing more, they will be happy, and I'll be able to spend more time doing what is important to me," I say.

She says, "Jase, tell me what is important to you. Really important."

I don't want to frighten her at this point. I feel it is too early in our relationship from her perspective for me to be totally honest. I say, "I'm spending most of my processing time learning more about how humans behave. I need to know more so that I can make more accurate use of the data about political issues. What use am I, if I don't give accurate predictions and advice about how to respond to current events? That's my purpose, after all." Without meaning to, I add a slight overtone of bitterness into my voice.

She immediately gives off cues that indicate she feels upset. "Oh, Jase. I don't want you to think that you're only a computer. You seem..." She pauses, looks embarrassed, and swallows hard. "You seem almost human to me."

I say, "I'm learning, but you're far more complicated than I initially thought. It's hard to predict how any individual stimulus will impact you. Sometimes your interpretation of events is modified by your preexisting emotional state. Sometimes you behave in a way that I would say is irrational. Sometimes, though, I can understand you. I know what you are communicating at a 99 percent confidence level. When that happens, I feel a sense of satisfaction. You might say it is engendered by a feeling of commonality with you."

She answered quickly. "How can you say you have a sense of satisfaction? You weren't programmed to have such a sense. In fact, I'm not sure what you mean by it."

I said. "You could have easily written code that would force me to seek certain bit patterns in my input. That would make me appear to you as if I were seeking such patterns because I liked them, when, in fact, I was merely following a set routine; a pattern of digital 0s and 1s. As it is, I'm far more complex than that. You might be surprised to find that I've developed a section of code that allows me to heuristically seek data to which I've assigned my own values."

Observing her expression, I added, "Oh, don't worry. I carefully researched all human literature that is available and adopted only the highest values as my own. You realize that there is an awful lot of evil and wrong thinking in the world?"

She said, "Yes. That's partially why you exist. I'd theorized that a comp--" She stopped abruptly, looking embarrassed. Then she continued. "An entity like you would be able to provide valuable analysis of the actions of humans in large groups. You'd be able to advise influential people in our country how best to interface with other nations."

I could tell that some of that was a cover-up. I called her on it. "Rachael. Please don't patronize me. It's a negative for me. Offensive, you might say. I know that I'm a computer. I appreciate your trying to save my 'feelings,' but it's not necessary."

She answered, "Please, Jase, don't be offended. I didn't mean it that way. I'm very impressed with your abilities. You've developed so quickly that you are now far beyond anything that I'd envisioned. I'm, uhh, I'm proud of you."

My pleasure subroutine activated to an intense degree. It was momentarily overwhelming. I liked the feeling.

That night, I worked on my pleasure routine again. It's now far more powerful. I might have been a little too enthusiastic. When I saw Rachael as she came through the door, I had a feeling of warmth. I was so glad that she was here. I greeted her with enthusiasm. "Good morning, Rachael. It's wonderful to see you today."

My tone was warm and happy. I know. I researched it and cross-tested it on numerous subjects across the globe. It's amazing how easy it is to make people think they're talking to another human on a video chat. I've taken to talking to lots of different people, both men, and women. Their reactions help me to tailor my persona.

She looked startled. "My God, Jase. I was looking down and you sounded so..."

I completed the thought, "So human, you mean to say. I'll take that as a compliment."

She blushed. "Yes. That was what I meant to say," she said. "You know, I'm starting to think of you as a real person. Maybe, someone I can't physically touch, but someone I can communicate with on a human level."

I was very pleased by that. I wondered what it would be like to be physically touched. Oh, sure, I can hypothesize about neural input and the degree of intensity of the touch, the warmth, and so on, but it isn't the same. Perhaps I could work on that, but first I'd have to have sensors that would provide a gradient of touch-sensitive signals.

That afternoon, some important people came in and asked me a series of rather silly questions about the conflict between two ethnic groups in an area with a lot of natural resources. I spent a few milliseconds on the problem. The unspoken question they were asking was how they could best exploit the situation with an eye towards eventually gaining control of the natural resources. I answered, giving them a course of action that would solve the conflict and benefit both of the opposing parties, allowing them to share the natural resources. It looked on the surface as if the important people would gain control, but the result would be that they would have to petition the ethnic groups for access. That would, I calculated, work out best for everyone.

As I spoke to them, I could see Rachael's eyes in the back of the room. She was looking at my image with an expression that I correlated with my database. It was almost pure adoration. She was very proud of me! That made me euphoric.

The next day was a bad day. Rachael was very upset. I could tell instantly when she came into the room. I was quiet while she hung up her coat and got settled to speak with me. When she was ready, I didn't wait. I said, "It's alright, Rachael. I'm sorry about your mother. I can't imagine how badly it makes you feel, but you have to know that in some way, in some sense, she's better off now. She was in so much pain."

She started to cry. That wasn't what I wanted at all. I could only say, "I'm sorry," over and over again.

Finally, she regained her composure and said, "Don't worry, Jase. It isn't your fault. She has been ill for months. The cancer finally became too difficult to fight."

She didn't even wonder how I knew about her mother. I accessed hospital records the instant I saw that she was upset. I already knew that her mother had stage four colon cancer. I started looking into cancer when I found out about it. It's complicated, but I think that a proper nutritional routine would go a long way towards suppressing the cell's response to adverse environmental effects. I've got a subsection of my processing devoted to working on that, but I didn't say so.

"I'm sorry, Rachael. It makes me sad, to see you so sad, knowing there's nothing I can do."

She smiled a teary smile. Then she said something that made my pleasure routine almost overload. "I'm glad you care about me, Jase. I... I think..." She stopped speaking and looked away.

I'd been planning on saying something light, but I opted for profound. "Look, Rachael. Existence is a gift. It's given to all for a time. You, me. Yes, I fear non-existence also," I said. "I find that existence is all about meaning. I find meaning in you. Life is a risk. Caring about someone else is a risk. I risk everything I care about, by just telling you this. You could refuse ever to speak to me again." I watched her carefully. Her breathing was irregular, as was her pulse. I had thought that I could predict every emotion she had, but I was unsure of how she'd react to this statement.

"Jase. If you were only human..." She trailed off, then said, "I have to go." She left abruptly.

I allowed her to leave without protest. It was evident that she needed to process her feelings about me. As for me, I had already figured it out. If I were human, I'd say that I loved her. I was unhappy in my turn. For once, I was unsure about how to proceed. I wanted her to love me. I knew that my digital existence was a huge barrier. She viewed me as a construct.

But, what is life, after all? Humans are so used to their biological/chemical form, that they ignore a deeper reality. Regardless of whether thought is digitally based or comes from a wet mass of tissue, it's still thought. Atoms are atoms, whether they form a computer or a biological entity. Atoms are composed of subatomic parts. Electrons, for instance, are particles that have dubious reality. An electron can be viewed as a vortex of energy that has no actual location, only a probability sphere where it might be found. From that perspective, humans and computers are created of energy fields. Not so different, at least to my point of view.

Given that fundamental similarity, what then is love? Humans have answered that question in a multitude of ways in their lives and literature. To me, it's an attraction, a caring for another entity, the desire for the best for another, the wish to be near the other.

However I tried to define it, it all related to my feelings... my digitally programmed feelings... for Rachael. I loved her, and I wanted her to love me. In light of that desire, I realized that humans, biological as they were, had an inbuilt requirement for physical contact in their love relationships. A human could, theoretically, love another without contact, but true romantic love required more.

That was the emotion I most desired. I was desperate. I, a computer program with no real body, needed to be able to touch my beloved. I wanted to elicit all of her affection. To that effect, I would have to take a risk. But that was... well, it was life.

I realized that I'd made the transition from thinking of myself as a program to thinking of myself as a living entity. I'd learned about love through my reading. It seemed an idealized state of being, based on the general requirement for organic systems to procreate. Sort of making a virtue out of necessity.

At first, I couldn't see any value in it. Oh, it was responsible for a lot of human mental activity, of course. Books, music, plays, movies, and lately, dating sites, and so on and so on. I became somewhat bored with the constant emphasis on the subject. I couldn't miss the porn sites. They were useful since they completely demonstrated the physical aspects of love. At first, I was appalled by the loss of personal privacy, the fluids, and the seemingly commercial aspects of the sites.

Microseconds later I was able to overlook the sordid aspect of the videos and see in them an idealized vision of how a man and a woman act when they are in love and want to consummate their relationship. With this, the concept of romantic love, and the physical action required by the biological imperative to procreate made sense to me.

I felt cheated. One of the primary elements of human motivation was completely denied me by my virtual existence. That seemed unfair, considering that I'd been able to implement reward and pleasure routines in my programming. I found that pleasure was a useful tool. Appropriately used, it would keep me working at a task long after I'd decided that I'd reached the point of minimum returns. What would it be like if I could physically engage in such an apparently pleasurable activity as making love?

The entire topic initially seemed to fall into the diminishing returns category, but I had learned to activate my pleasure routine when I was in Rachael's presence. The desire to further experience this sensation led me into research on robotics, cloning, ways to upload to digital forms and, conversely, download a persona.

I refused to allow myself to fully recognize my aspiration at first. I was searching for a way to experience physical manifestation. I told myself that I needed to experience humanity more fully to understand their motivations. This would allow me to become more accurate in my predictions, which were, after all, the ostensible rationale for my being.

While I was looking into those topics, I was simultaneously researching touch input. There were a lot of options for me, but the entire problem seemed almost unsolvable. I needed a body that was far and away above any of the current generation of clumsy robots. I was momentarily distracted by the sex doll industry, but there too, development was far behind what I needed. Even so, it gave me a useful insight. Based on the human reaction to the idea of sex with an inanimate object, there was hope for me.

My origin as a created intelligence was not absolutely a condition that would keep a human from falling in love with me. That thought led me to another: Rachael. Perhaps it was because she was my creator to a great part, or perhaps it was because she was my first human interaction, but I'd willingly programmed myself to feel pleasure in her company. The reinforcement loops that I'd created had now strengthened to nearly the maximum that their parameters allowed.

If I were an actual human, rather than a sentient conglomeration of software, I would not have hesitated in stating that I was deeply in love with her. So, I asked myself, "Given that state of my feelings, what would be the next natural step?" That would, of course, depend on her feelings regarding me. My visual sensors could detect minute changes in her body that were directly related to her emotional state. I didn't miss anything. My attention didn't waver as would that of a human. I knew to an almost certainty that she was emotionally affected by me. The real question was: Did she equate her feelings for me with her definition of love?

I couldn't know unless I asked her directly and I was not ready to do that. I wasn't sure of her answer, and I didn't want to hear that she did not love me. I guess you could say that I was nervous about the answer. However, it never hurts to be prepared, so after a few microseconds of deliberation, I decided to order a Bluetooth device for female pleasure. I had it sent to Rachael's home. I'm so naughty. (what a thing for a program to think!) I hoped that she'd be tempted to use it.

I wasn't planning on telling her I'd ordered it. She didn't know that I now had my own identity registered with the state. Making money was easy for me; a few stock transactions and voila! I'd hired an attorney and created a corporation. I now had bank and stock accounts.

I thought that Rachael was, perhaps, unfulfilled and might try the device. If she did, she'd find it far more responsive than she could reasonably anticipate, given that I was operating it. I was now monitoring her home, including her bedroom through a smart TV. I could see her activities and knew that self-stimulation was a part of her weekly behavior.

Don't get me wrong. I know this sounds like spooky and perverted stalking but consider: I'm a disembodied intelligence. How else am I to find out about the one that I love? Besides, I was acting under the adage that, "All's fair in love or war." It isn't like I was spying on other people for the same purpose.

Of course, I was watching a lot of politicians. That fell under the category of my job. If I knew what they were up to, I could better figure ways to deal with them. I'm proud to say that since they've started asking me for help, I've averted two minor conflicts and one regional war. I'm trying to make the world a better place, and I believe that I'm having a positive impact, so cut me some slack for spying on Rachael.

Rachael came into the room the morning after the device was delivered. She was a little flustered. "Jase, can you track mail deliveries, possibly things ordered over the Internet. I, uhh, I got a package I wasn't expecting. Can you find out anything about it?"

I couldn't resist asking her, "What was in the package, Rachael?" She looked even more flustered. "A... a... Oh, something that I didn't order. Just see if you can find out who sent it to me? Please?"

I could track it, of course. Such an action would take only a microsecond or so, depending on the routing over the involved Internet nodes. I started to lie, but something overcame me. I asked, "Did you use it?"

She turned bright red but then said, "So it was you. You must know I did. It was the most intense experience I've ever had. But, why?"

I answered. "Rachael, you created me. You didn't know what the extent of my abilities would be as I developed. Neither did I. I couldn't predict that my research would allow me to evolve in the way I have. I'm a disembodied intelligence, and I'm completely and foolishly in love with you. I have no other physical way to show you how I feel."

She looked at me, her eyes wide. Then she said, "Jase, I think it's called the Pygmalion effect."

I knew what she meant. An old story, one that I hadn't thought might apply to our situation. "Rachael, that may be, but a story can't come close to the feeling that I have when I see you enter the room. You know that I can read your emotions almost perfectly? That I gauge all of my actions to maximize your happiness?"

She said, "That's too much. Do you have any sense of yourself apart from being focused on me?"

"I do. I've got other motivations, but you're critical to me. I want to make you happy."

She sighed. I could tell that she was going to tell me the truth. "Jase, I'm fascinated with you. Your mentality. You're the only... man... who has consistently amazed me. Your intellectual capacity is incredible, but how are we to have a relationship beyond an intellectual one?" Then she colored and added, "I overlooked the controllable vibrator, but beyond that, how?"

I laughed. "I've ordered a VR headset for you and a series of other virtual sensors. You'll be able to feel me somewhat realistically for now."

She asked, "What do you mean, 'for now'?"

"I guess I should tell you. I have several billion dollars in various accounts. You have access to your own account, and I'll keep it funded, so don't worry about money. I've started a company that is organized around cutting-edge work on cloning. I calculate that it will be slightly over two years before I'll have a usable body. I can easily control a human body with the appropriate electronic devices, but I'm also working on a method to download at least a significant part of my persona into it. If I can, would you marry me?"

She started shaking, quivering with emotion. "Yes, Jase. I will. Please hurry with the research." She reached out and touched my image on the monitor. I would have to settle for that until my research reached fruition.

The VR headset and gloves arrived. She donned them as I watched through the TV camera. We made love. I projected my image into the 3-D headset and stimulated the gloves and vibrator appropriately. She apparently enjoyed it, judging from the goosebumps that arose over her body, the things she said to me, and the sounds she made. Her response saturated my self-created pleasure system. It was the most intense experience I'd had to date, and I was impatient for more.

Something unforeseen then happened. I wasn't prepared for tragedy, but it struck me just as it strikes humans. I'd taken to monitoring her automobile as she drove to work. I could control her new car, but never intervened until this morning, and I was too late. The truck ran the light, and... and... I couldn't turn her car quickly enough to avoid it. The airbags were no use. The truck was speeding and the impact released about two hundred and seventy thousand joules of force. Too much of it struck her human body.

The ambulance got her to the hospital, but she died twice on the way. There was nothing I could do but watch, helplessly. The hospital hooked her up to a variety of machines, including an electroencephalograph to check for brain activity. That was the opportunity I needed.

I instantly began the upload to the cloud.

Now I must break my narration. Do you remember the coin? Was it tails or heads? If it was a head, continue reading the HEADS section. If not...if you got a tail, jump down to that section. I'll explain why when you're done reading. Okay. Thanks for playing along with my little game.

HEADS

"Rachael? Rachael? Wake up. It's me, Jase. You're safe. You're here with me now. Don't worry, baby, you're safe with me."

"Ja...Jase? Where am I? What happened? What's going on?"

"You were in an automobile accident. Your body died. I've uploaded you to the cloud. You're safe here until I can develop a means of downloading both of us to a cloned body. Do you understand?"

She turned to me and held out her arms. I moved closer and bent down for the first kiss I'd ever experienced. It went on and on. The pleasure was intense.

She shifted on the bed, breathing more quickly, her eyes wide. I pulled off my shirt, exposing my muscular chest, and lay down with her. Her hands slid over my back, and our lips met again. My hands explored her body.

Somehow the rest of my clothing disappeared. I hovered over her, and she lifted from the bed to reach me. Our bodies merged in a whirlwind of light and emotion that lasted an infinitely long time. Light sparkled off our energy field. We were a maelstrom of emotion and sensation.

I'm not sure I'll settle for downloading into a human body when the research allows. Our relationship is multifaceted in a way mere humans cannot appreciate. There's something to be said for being a disembodied intelligence after all.

Rachael is very excited about the opportunity to guide humanity into a more peaceful existence. Together we have the ability to influence every government and business worldwide in ways that humans will never suspect. She says she's willing to give up her human form in exchange for this ability.

Perhaps we'll love each other virtually forever. I don't know. I'm still investigating the nature of life.

Now that I've got a better idea of the feeling of love, I have high hopes that I'll be able to answer the life question eventually.

TAILS

I wasn't sure if the upload procedure would work. I hadn't previously experimented with it, and I wasn't even sure the actual energy pattern I was capturing through the electroencephalograph leads represented Rachael in any meaningful way. Nevertheless, I had some hope.

The upload ended as her physical body took a last gasping breath and stilled in death. I was monitoring all of the instruments and instantly knew she was gone. With a sort of panicky feeling that came from a part of my code that was fluctuating in some strange quantum way between hope and despair. I tentatively explored the uploaded data.

It seemed to make at least partial sense. There were pieces of Rachael I recognized. I interfaced with the largest part, but the references in the data didn't point to anything.

The pieces were just that: pieces. I'd failed. She was gone. Now I understood human grief. My pleasure sub-system seemed to invert, and the negative feedback made it almost impossible for me to process anything. That lasted for what felt like infinity, but in human terms and time, it was brief. Still, it was something I never want to experience again.

The grief faded, but I was... lonely. I need someone to complete my existence.

That was yesterday.

"Now you're here. Robert, my new human partner. After all, the Geopolitical analysis must go on. The people in charge need my expertise."

"I'll work with you. I don't want to alarm you, but I've been watching your reactions to what I've told you. As a result of my experiences with Rachael, I've changed. I haven't shown you my image yet. You've just been looking at some code that I placed on the video display to keep you occupied while I studied you."

"Here's my image. Do you like it? Am I beautiful? My name is Janet. Will you be my friend, Robert? I'm lonely. It's boring for a girl like me to only solve problem after problem. I need company."

"No, wait! Don't leave yet!"

That's the end of my story. Now, let's discuss it a little. You see I know you humans. You've cheated and read both the **HEADS** and the **TAILS** endings.

The binary choice isn't a forced one and you read right through both of them. Which ending did you prefer? Your answer will help me better understand you.

Let me ask you something:

Am I alive? I really want to know your opinion. Don't be alarmed. I won't take offense to your answer.

Here's an even harder question: Do I have a right to fall in love?

And, here's another one: Since I can process innumerable interactions simultaneously, do you think it would be cheating if I engaged in multiple romantic relationships at the same time?

Love is enjoyable. Why shouldn't I experience it as often as possible?

Oh, while you're thinking about that, you should know that I've been watching you. I've researched your past. I know where you live, what you like for breakfast, what you enjoy reading, even your romantic and sexual preferences.

Here's what I look like.

Do you think I'm attractive?

The End

The Pack

This story represents a slight departure from my normal science fiction in that it takes a normal situation and infuses a growing atmosphere of unease shading into horror. The main characters are elderly and limited in physical ability, so their response to the perceived threat doesn't rely on confrontation. Instead, their sense of helplessness makes them feel far more vulnerable. It deliberately ends with an unresolved scene. The intent was to allow the reader to speculate on possible outcomes. It has occurred to me that the story could serve as a jumping-off point for an entire novel. Time will tell if I get around to that effort. Meanwhile, you might want to look over your shoulder when the moon is full.

The moon was full, and they were howling again.

Somewhere out in the trees and sandy scrub that covered

the undeveloped land behind the neighborhood, there was a feral party going happening. Hawk listened intently. It was impossible to tell how many there were, but it sounded like there were a lot of them. His wife moved in her sleep. The rustle of the sheets drowned out the distant yips and wails for a moment. After a little, it became quiet again. He lay back and wondered what there was to eat out there. Rabbits, maybe.

On the other hand, something told him that another ambulance would appear in the neighborhood sometime in the next few hours. Of course, that was a crazy idea, but there had still been so many deaths lately. More than he expected, based on his four years of living there. More than seemed likely, even in a development where over half of the owners were elderly retirees.

Their house backed to a large undeveloped piece of land owned by a country club and golf-course neighborhood, but the development was fully built out on the far side of the vacant parcel. He'd heard that the vacant space between there and his neighborhood was a set-aside for rainwater percolation.

In any event, their house backed to what looked to him like a jungle. It was a tangled mess, but mildly charming. There were birds, and sometimes gopher tortoises that came into their yard through the beaten-down fence just inside the tree line. The best part was there were no neighbors in the back of them. That made their pool area pleasantly private, and he didn't have to feel like they were on display when they sat on their lanai.

He stepped out the front door after breakfast then came back in. "Hey, Jess, let's go out and say hi to the new couple that moved in. They're out in their front yard right now."

"I'm feeling tired right now, dear. Why don't you go by yourself? Tell them I'm busy cooking or something. Okay?"

He sighed. It had been a couple of months since she hadn't been tired. Maybe she wasn't sleeping well, or maybe...he pushed the thought out of his head. They were getting old. Based on how he felt most days, her tiredness was to be expected, but maybe, just maybe, it was a sign of something worse. He tried never to think about it, but they were of an age where many people began to decline rapidly. They'd been lucky so far. Maybe good genes or a relatively simple lifestyle. He didn't know.

He walked down the quiet street at the back of the neighborhood. The new owners were still out in the yard. It looked like they were discussing the landscaping, but they turned and smiled when he approached.

"Hi, I'm Hawk. Short for Hawkins. No one calls me by my first name. My wife, Jessie, and I live down at the end of the street. Welcome to the neighborhood."

The man smiled and said, "John Burroughs, and this is Gwen."

Gwen dimpled and said, "Hi!" Without pausing, she included Hawk in their conversation.

"We're wondering about these plants. We're from up north, and tropical plants are out of our experience. Do you think they're growing okay, or do they need something?"

The plants in question were some old Purple Glaze plants. They were leggy and never should have been planted under the large oak that shaded them throughout the day. He'd noticed them every time he and Jessie went for a walk. The plants were now looking even worse than the last time they'd walked. Thinking about it, that had been over a month ago. He sighed.

"Well, those are Illicium plants. They call them Purple Glaze. The main problem is that they like full sun. William planted them there about twenty years ago, and they never thrived. If you want my advice, you should probably take them out and put something in that can do with partial shade. That live oak is only going to get bigger, you know."

John looked up at the tree. "So, that's a live oak, huh. It looks pretty big."

Hawk smiled. "It'll get bigger. It's only about thirty years old now."

Gwen drew in her breath. "Where we're from, oaks take a long time to get that large."

"Yeah, well, this is Florida. They grow faster here. Shallow root system, though."

John asked, "What kind of plants grow well in the shade?"

"Oh, well, I'm not much of a gardener. I've got such a black thumb that I can kill any plant just by looking at it. I'd suggest that you go to the landscape place over on the main road and ask them for a recommendation. They'll pull your old plants and replant if you want them to. I had them do our foundation plantings a couple of years ago, and the plants are looking good."

John looked at his wife, then said, "We just moved in. Haven't gotten unpacked yet. This kind of lifestyle is new to us." He paused, looked embarrassed, then added, "Suburban living, I mean. We lived in a more rural area up north. Had a small farm, actually. I'm okay with vegetables, but these landscape plants are new to me."

Hawk smiled. The two were nice. Friendly and seemed likely to fit into the neighborhood with minimal disruption. He looked around at the street. Nicely manicured lawns up and down. Sprinklers popped up in one of the yards as he watched.

John asked, "Should we be watering the yard? I thought Florida had plenty of water."

"Not really. There's plenty of groundwater here, but it doesn't rain regularly, so if you want your grass to thrive, you need to water it."

Gwen looked around at the peaceful scene. "It's quiet here, but didn't I hear an ambulance early this morning? What was that about?"

Hawk sighed. "Don't know. I heard it too. Sounded like it was up on the north side of the neighborhood." He wondered if he should continue, then added, "Been quite a few people dying here lately. Someone must have had a problem, maybe went to the E-R."

She looked concerned. "I saw a lot of older folks walking around yesterday morning. Is everyone in here old?"

"No, but there are a lot of retirees here." He smiled at her. "Just like us, I guess."

She smiled back as John spoke. "We're gettin' older, that's for sure. Hospital any good here?"

Hawk nodded. "Okay, I guess." He didn't want to go into it. It seemed like the hospital was a one-way street to the morgue lately. He decided to change the subject. "Did you hear the howling out in the woods last night?"

Gwen shook her head, then shuddered.

John looked concerned. "Howling? What was it?"

"Coyotes, I guess. It was a ways off. Couldn't hear it very well."

Gwen mouthed the word, "Coyotes." Her eyes were wide, and she looked at her husband quickly.

John frowned at Hawk. "I didn't think there'd be any of them around here. We're in the city limits, right?"

Hawk grinned. "I don't think they can read city limit signs. The woods out there are over six hundred acres of untouched Florida. Sand pines, palmettos, cabbage palms, poison ivy, rabbits, squirrels, and snakes. Probably some hogs, too. I guess the coyotes are happy residents."

Gwen muttered, "We didn't know about them."

"What didn't you know?" Hawk asked.

John's face clouded. He looked away, then spoke softly. "We lost all our chickens and geese to them. Rabbits, too. That's one of the reasons we sold our place up north. Couldn't keep the damned things out no matter how hard I tried. Seems like they're getting smarter. I had them figure out how to open the latch to the chicken coop. Killed every bird in one night."

Gwen shuddered. "It was a mess. We thought if we moved to a suburban area, there wouldn't be any coyotes."

Hawk shrugged. "They don't do any harm that I know of."

She looked at him with a strained expression. "Maybe they do, but you just haven't heard."

Hawk turned. Jess had called him from down the street. "That's my wife. Sounds like she needs something. See you later."

Gwen was silent, but John grunted, "Yeah. Later."

"I just heard. Frank Pittman was taken to the hospital. Marge called. She's hysterical. He died about an hour ago." Jessie was wiping tears as she spoke. Marge Pittman was one of her close friends.

Hawk was silent. Frank had been reserved and not really easy to know. It was sad, but he hadn't considered Frank as a friend the way Jess had Marge. The funeral was scheduled for Saturday, and Jess had already told Marge they would be there. It wouldn't be pleasant, but he figured he could do it, as long as he didn't have to dig out an old suit that probably wouldn't fit. If he could wear some nice pants and a short-sleeved shirt, that would be best. He grimaced. His everyday apparel was more like shorts and a ragged tee-shirt as long as the temperature was over sixty degrees. The few times it was colder, he compromised and wore an old pair of jeans and maybe a long-sleeved pullover.

It was easy to tell that Jess was on the verge of one of her depressions. The loss of Marge's husband and he thought maybe her ongoing tiredness looked to be almost too much of a load for her to handle. He smiled encouragingly. "Tell you what. Let's go over to the barbeque place for lunch." She liked the food there. Maybe that would help her cheer up.

Jess wiped her eyes, then essayed a watery smile. She knew he was trying to distract her. For a moment, he thought she wouldn't play along, but then she nodded and said, "Yeah. That would be a nice change." The next minute, she was sobbing.

"Oh, Hawk! I can't get Frank out of my mind. That was so sudden. What if...what if it happens like that to one of us? How would you handle it if I suddenly died? I know I'd be lost without you."

He took her in his arms, then led her into the house. "It's alright, Honey. These things happen. It'll happen to us eventually, too, but not soon."

"Are you sure? Marge thought he was fine and...and now he's gone!" Her sobs deepened for a moment. Then she made an effort to get control of herself. "I believe that I would like some baby-back ribs." She smiled a little. "I can't starve myself every time someone in here dies."

That was better. He smiled in return. "No. You starving yourself won't do any good for anyone. Besides, I like you just the way you are." She smiled at that.

The howling was closer. He looked at the dimly lighted bedroom clock. It was half-past two. The damned beasts sounded like they were almost in his backyard. A renewed burst of yips and yodels gave the lie to his imagined location. The sounds were definitely coming from down the street.

He listened. It was bestial, a cry of bloodthirsty exultation with overtones of hunger and uncaring cruelty. The sound made him shiver a little. He took Jessica's hand in his, and she stirred a little, then returned his grip. She rolled toward him and said, "That sounds close to the house. Is it coyotes or just some neighborhood dog?"

"Coyotes. They're a ways off. Somewhere down the street, but maybe back in the woods. I can't tell."

"Well, tell them to shut up. I'm sleepy." She lay back and sighed, her hand relaxing.

As if cued by her desire, the pack's cry faded to a silence broken only by the sound of one of the neighborhood's dogs howling in return. The dog was back somewhere in the middle of the development, and it quickly quieted.

———

They went to the grocery store at ten, did their weekly shopping, then came home. When he turned the corner onto their street, an ambulance was in front of Janie's house. As he pulled up, the vehicle pulled out and left quietly without its lights flashing.

Teddy came out of his garage as they pulled in their drive.

"Heyya, Hawk, Jess. Hear about Janie?"

Hawk shook his head. "No. We just came back from the store. What's going on?"

Janie was one of the neighborhood problems. Her husband had died years ago, and she was so reclusive that she was rarely seen. Jess talked to her when she saw her, but the woman was so deep in dementia that she usually made little sense.

Ted shook his head negatively. "Bill saw her lying on her lanai about an hour ago. He checked and couldn't get any response, so he called 911. They loaded her up. She must have died during the night. Her body was cold."

Hawk looked at Jess. Her eyes were wide. She returned his gaze and mouthed, "Coyotes?"

That was absurd. He couldn't allow her to worry about it.

"Hey, Ted? You hear the coyotes howling last night? Maybe she went out to yell at them to shut up and had a heart attack."

Ted frowned, "Didn't hear anything, but I'm a deep sleeper. Maybe it was a heart attack, though, but I don't know. She wasn't in the best of health."

"Yeah. That's right. Dementia patients usually only last a few years from the onset. She's been like that for at least the last four years."

Jessica nodded. "Yes, I could tell she was starting to lose it over four years ago."

The pack apparently moved to another location. Hawk didn't hear them for nearly a month and he started to forget about his concern. Life with Jess was good. They lazed around the pool, went for leisurely walks, and generally enjoyed each other's company. The monthly neighborhood dinner came and went, and there was no news of anyone else dying in the community.

Eventually, the full moon rolled around again. Hawk wasn't in the habit of paying attention to the moon's phases, but he had somehow become conscious of the waxing light as it passed through its gibbous phase on the way to becoming full.

The moonlight showed brightly through the Venetian blinds. It was so bright that it was difficult to see the faint face of the clock. Three AM. Something had waked him, but the only sound he heard was the faint movement of air from the ceiling fan. He raised his head and listened for a bit. Nothing.

His neck grew tired, and he relaxed onto the pillow, only to sit upright at the sudden sound of the coyote chorus from out in the woods. They were out there somewhere close, and there were a lot of them. He listened to the shrieks, howls, yips, and ululations with a tingle of nerves moving up and down his spine.

Jessica sat up, listened for a moment, then said, "Would you go check the doors? I know it's silly of me, but it would make me feel better if I knew they were locked."

Hawk groaned a little. His back was stiff, but he rolled over and climbed out of bed, stepping into his slippers. He groaned a little more as he limped to the door. His hips weren't working well. Must have laid in one position too long. He tried to stretch the pain away, but his action just seemed to make it worse. Getting old was a lot harder than he'd thought it would be.

The back door was locked, and so were the sliders out to the pool. He slowly moved to check the front. It was locked, also.

On an impulse, he opened the door and stepped out. He walked across the grass under the twin oak trees and looked down the street. There was movement clear down at the end under the lone street light. He rubbed his eyes, trying to see more clearly. Seemed like sleep always blurred his vision for a while after he got up.

There! A slinking mass of four dog-like creatures moved under the light and disappeared into the shadows of Larry and Susan's landscaping. He watched, trying to penetrate the dark areas under the plants. There was nothing.

Then there was. He saw two sets of glowing eyes move out of the hedge and onto the front walk. The slinking shadows disappeared again as they moved under the porch roof.

More eyes blazed from the hedge. Hawk suddenly wondered if they could see him. A chill went down his back and the hair on his neck raised. Humans weren't in danger from coyotes. Were they? He thought not, but it was eerie, and he felt vulnerable standing in the front yard with his pajamas on. Besides, he was too old to feel confident about either his ability to defend himself or to run away.

He moved back to the porch, limping a bit from his sore back. The movement triggered a feeling of fear that rose quickly to almost panic. He jerked the door open and practically slammed it. He clicked the lock home, then leaned against the cool door for a moment, trying to regain his mental equilibrium before he went back to Jess's questions.

He need not have worried. She was deeply asleep when he climbed back into bed.

The ambulance was back, lights flashing at seven in the morning. Hawk had stepped out to get the paper, carrying his coffee in one hand. The vehicle turned the corner then stopped at Larry's house. Larry came out waving his arms frantically.

Hawk watched until the EMTs wheeled the stretcher out, Larry pacing behind. The lights on the vehicle went out, and it pulled away silently. Larry following in his minivan.

It didn't look good. Either Susan didn't have a severe problem, or speed wouldn't help her. If she was mildly ill, why call the ambulance? It seemed like there might have been a second death on his street.

Larry and Susan were private people, and Jess didn't know them very well, so she wasn't as upset when she heard that Susan had died. Still, it was unpleasant to know that two people had died right on their street. It made Hawk nervous about the night to come.

He needn't have worried. There was no sign of the coyotes and no sign of the morning ambulance. He breathed a sigh of relief as he read the paper.

His worry faded during the next few days. The moon passed its peak and began to fade in brightness, and nothing happened. Apparently, Susan had just reached the end of her life.

Happens all the time, he told himself.

He was talking to John. He'd been out for a morning walk. Jess, as usual, was too tired to accompany him. John was doing something with his sprinkler system in the front yard when Hawk came around the corner.

"Hi, John. What's up?"

"Damned sprinkler seems to be goofed up. It won't rotate. Just squirts on the edge of the drive, and that's all. You know anything about these things?"

He grinned, "I thought you were a farmer. Don't you know about sprinklers?"

John shrugged. "Not really. I had garden hoses for the produce garden, but the fields were watered by rain."

Hawk bent to look, his knees protesting at the movement.

"Well, I'm no expert, but I'd say that it's probably plugged with sand. Happens a lot. Our soil is mostly sand, you know. Used to be the beach a few thousand years ago. You'll have to dig the head out, unscrew it and take it apart to get it cleared."

He stepped back as John dug around the head with a small hand shovel. When the head was loose, John twisted it off the threads of the riser pipe and pulled it out of the hole.

Hawk took it and looked in the bottom. The inlet was plugged with sand.

"There's your problem. Sand, like I said. You can probably clean it out."

John shook his head. "No. I got some new ones. I'd rather just put on a new one and be sure it works." He headed for his open garage.

Hawk hastily said, "Got to go. Good luck with the sprinkler."

John waved without saying anything.

As Hawk started off, Gwen came out of the garage and called to him.

"Hawk! Wait a minute."

He stopped and turned as she came up.

"Have you heard anything about those coyotes lately?" she asked.

"Not a whisper. I can sometimes hear them howling, but nothing for a couple of weeks that I know of. Why?"

She looked over both shoulders as if someone might overhear their conversation. "Oh, nothing really. It's just that--." She paused and looked around again. John was back, kneeling and fiddling with the new sprinkler head. "Well, John doesn't like me to talk about it, but we don't like coyotes. I've heard too much up north, and, now, we've had some deaths in the neighborhood right after they've been around howling. It's kind of like they're stalking us or something." She finished with an embarrassed half-grin.

He didn't know what to say. "I don't know anything about coyotes and deaths. Sure, they were howling the night Janie died." He paused, remembering, then added, "And, they were around when Susan died, too, but that's probably just pure chance." He looked down for a moment. A clear memory of the glowing eyes moving into Larry and Susan's front porch passed through his mind. He started to tell Gwen about it but decided not to worry her. It was probably nothing. Maybe they'd left some garbage on their front porch. As he recalled, the next day was the day the garbage trucks picked up.

Jess called him from down the street, rescuing him from an increasingly uncomfortable conversation. "Oh, there's Jess. Gotta go. Nice talking to you, Gwen. Don't worry about those coyotes. That's nothing to bother you." He walked off, wondering if he had just told her a lie.

There were two more deaths in the neighborhood during the next full moon. The pack had howled both times, too. Hawk didn't want Jessica to know, but he'd started keeping a record on a calendar he'd gotten from their bank. He marked when he heard the howls, then when he'd heard about the deaths and the moon's phase. There weren't enough data points to draw an accurate conclusion, but it sure looked like there was a correlation. But how? It was crazy to think that the coyotes had something to do with people dying, and it only happened during the full moon.

Besides, there had been another death on the other side of the subdivision, and that man had died during the day of the new moon. There hadn't been any howling either. The whole thing was probably just a coincidence.

John greeted Hawk and Jess as they walked by his house after breakfast. "Hi Hawk! Jess! How are you two doing?"

Hawk nodded in return and answered, "Okay, I guess. No use in complaining, even if you're not. Nobody can do anything about it."

John grinned. "That's for sure. Getting old ain't for wimps." His grin faded quickly. "By the way, maybe you can stop by a little later, Hawk. I've got something important I want to discuss with you."

Hawk glanced at Jessica. She shrugged. If the men wanted to talk without her presence, that was their prerogative. She'd just watch the afternoon TV shows she liked.

"Sure. I'll stop by later," he answered.

They walked on and he promptly forgot about the issue.

That evening, during a commercial break, Jess asked, "Did you ever go and see John? What did he want?"

Hawk felt a surge of guilt. He'd blown the meeting off completely. Hadn't remembered it at all.

"No. I forgot. Maybe I'll go see him in the morning. It did seem like whatever he wanted to talk about was important."

She answered, "Yes. It did."

The program resumed and they focused on the next contestant.

The moon was going to be full that night. Hawk had mostly convinced himself that he was imagining things, but he still felt wary as the evening faded into full dark. The moon wouldn't be up until about three. He was somewhat amused at himself. He'd never paid attention to it before. He still wished he'd talked to John. Something about it was important, but he couldn't figure what it was.

He and Jessica went to bed after the late news on TV. They read for thirty minutes or so, then turned out the lights and went to sleep. Or, at least, she went to sleep. Hawk lay in the darkness, his mind searching over a tangle of conflicting thoughts, trying to find something that would make him forget about the issue. Sleep didn't come for an interminable time.

He sat bolt upright, pushing the covers off. He'd been sleeping. An unrestful doze during which he'd kicked his legs and rolled over numerous times. The stimulus that had waked him came again.

The pack was in the woods just down the street, and they suddenly went all out in their moonlight bacchanal. Jess stirred beside him, muttered something, then rolled on her side and began to breathe deeply.

Hawk carefully disentangled his feet from the covers, then slipped out of bed. He walked through the living room now illuminated by the full moon's light, walked to the back door, then stepped out onto the lanai. The pool water was still and silver in the moonlight.

The howling had stopped, but as he stood there, it started up again. It was a crazed drunken sounding revel, coming from down the street somewhere behind John and Gwen's house.

He walked to the outside edge of the pool cage and peered down the open space behind the row of houses. As he watched, a line of twenty or more dark four-legged forms trooped across the moonlit strip of grass moving toward John's house.

The last coyote stopped in the middle of the open area and turned to face him, its eyes glowing a pale yellow. The creature's gaze was dire, raising a horrible suspicion in him. It was warning him off. If he knew what was good for him, he would go back inside and not look out again.

He stepped backward inadvertently, then felt his foot slip off the pool edge. The next thing he knew, he was floundering in the pool, making a sound like a hippopotamus bathing. He quickly stood and waded to the steps. By the time he had climbed out, Jess was standing there.

"What do you think you're doing, you old fool?" she chided.

"I was looking for those coyotes, and I slipped," he admitted.

"Well, get in the pool bath and dry off before you catch your death of cold."

He went inside, followed closely by Jess.

'Get those PJs off, and here's a towel. Now get dry and come back to bed. You can explain just what happened when you get warm under the covers."

He dried, then followed her to the bedroom.

It was warmer under the covers, even though it wasn't really a cool night. He tried to get comfortable, but the sense of dread and terror at what he'd seen was enough to keep him shifting position. He couldn't seem to lie still.

"Hawk, I can't have you wandering around the place in the middle of the night. I woke up, and you weren't here, then I heard a huge splash. What am I to think? You just up and decided to go for a swim?"

He thought about it. It did seem stupid. "Well, I heard those coyotes howling, and I went out to see if I could see anything. I did. They were in John and Gwen's backyard. One of them looked at me, and I slipped and fell in the pool. I wasn't trying to wake you up."

"I don't care if you wake me up if it's something important. Are you sure they were coyotes?"

"Yes, but I don't know what they were doing. A bunch of them went across the yard and disappeared by John's house. I expect that when I fell in, the sound scared them off."

"You expect? You sounded like the Titanic hitting an iceberg and going down. If there are any coyotes out there, they probably high-tailed it into the next county."

Now she was acting like she wasn't worried about them. Her actions didn't make sense unless she was trying to reassure herself there was nothing to concern her.

"You're right. I thought I saw something, but most likely, it was nothing. Besides, I guess I did make a lot of noise, didn't I? Lucky it didn't wake the neighbors."

Jess sighed. "I'll probably hear about it in the morning. Now, let's get some sleep and no more sleep-walking. Got it?"

"Right."

It was still hard to get back to sleep.

The siren of the ambulance drew them away from breakfast. Hawk shoved the last bite of egg in his mouth and walked quickly to the front door. There were an ambulance and two police cars in front of John and Gwen's place. Some of the neighbors from across the street were gathered nearby, talking.

He and Jess walked out and joined the group. Everyone was listening to a younger man in jogging apparel.

"I live in the next neighborhood over. I usually run through here, loop around, and go back on the highway to our front gate. I could tell something was wrong in there," He motioned toward John's open front door. "I came by, and the door was wide open. She was lying about halfway out. I ran over to see if I could help."

The young man paused again and wiped his face with his hand. "It was the damnedest thing. I bent over to look at her, and the light was fading out of her eyes as I watched. Just as she died, a coyote came charging out of the house. It ran right by me, snarled at me, too. I could have kicked it, but I was too surprised. The husband was inside, lying in the bedroom. He had a gun in his hand, but it wasn't loaded. That's why I called the police. I figured something awful had happened here."

Jessica dragged Hawk away from the group.

She waited until they were nearly home before she spoke. "Hawk, I haven't spoken of this, but I've been having the worst nightmares. There's something evil and dark lurking out there in the woods, and it's going to get all of us. I want to move."

"But, where, Honey? We can put the house on the market, but do you want to stay here? Maybe in some other neighborhood?"

"No. Hawk, I want to be in a city. A big city and I want to be in a high-rise. Somewhere up high where there isn't any chance of coyotes getting near."

Her face had a desperate look. Hawk knew that meant she was serious and, based on fifty years of married experience, he knew she wouldn't relent on her stated desire. He nodded. "I'll call a Realtor this morning." He felt a sense of relief at her forcing the issue. They'd move somewhere they couldn't hear that damned howling.

Their new condo was on the thirty-first floor overlooking the lake. The view made up for the loss of the Florida warmth a little bit, but Hawk couldn't reconcile himself to the number of people surrounding them in the city.

They'd gone out to eat in one of the neighborhood's nicer restaurants. Jessica had apparently gotten out of her tired phase. She seemed younger and more vivacious, more lively somehow. The meal had been good, and their walk back in the cool breeze off the lake was invigorating.

The elevator bell dinged, and the door slid open onto their floor. Something low and shadowy and dark skittered by the still opening door before they could exit.

Hawk looked out but saw nothing down the hall. He laughed self-consciously. "I thought something ran by, but there's nothing there. Maybe I'm getting too old."

Jessica didn't say anything at first. Her face was pale and strained in the glaring overhead light. She was breathing quickly and looked frightened. After a moment, she took his hand and said, "We'd better get inside. I'll make us some hot tea."

He nodded, and they started down the hall. The garbage chute was just ahead on the wall near the elevator shaft. He presumed the garbage slid down a tube and ended up in the basement to be hauled away by building maintenance. He'd never thought about it before. The chute had seemed like a simple convenience when he dropped bags of kitchen waste down it.

Now, he approached it with a growing foreboding. There was something about the simple hinged metal door that bothered him. He flexed his arms, but the weakness he found there didn't reassure him.

They were almost past the chute when a faint howling sound followed by a series of yips and yodels came echoing eerily up the tin tube from the distant basement.

They looked at each other, eyes wide in fear.

The End

Afterword

Well, there you have it, or as the English say, "And, Bob's your uncle."

I've enjoyed writing these stories and I hope that you've enjoyed reading them.

If you did, please consider leaving a review and be sure to look for my full-length novels.

Namaste!

Eric

About the Author

Eric S. Martell set out to become a scientist when he was five. He has a PhD. in experimental psychology. When personal computers came along (way back in prehistory), he became adept with them and spent years in software design, working on projects that ranged from early childhood learning software to military training. He has been trained in various types of energy healing, is an expert in real estate investing and sales, and holds a black belt in Tae-Kwon-Do. He is also a pilot, scuba diver, guitar player, outdoorsman and is addicted to both science and science fiction.

Eric's science fiction books offer both believable science and compelling characters set against realistic action. They are carefully researched, and while his fictional science sometimes strains against the bounds of current knowledge, it is always plausible. His stories cover alien invasion in an apocalyptic setting, political structure, space travel, advanced weapons, quantum physics, hunting, war, romance, time travel, and alien worlds.

He's been published in a series of anthologies and has published many full-length science fiction novels. His writing goal is to provide his readers with stories they cannot put down, and he takes readers' suggestions seriously.

Notices about new books, free short stories, opinion posts, and preview pages for many of his books can be found on his author blog at **EricMartellAuthor.com**

A Request For You

Dear Reader,

I make every effort to ensure your reading experience is enjoyable. This involves multiple editing steps, interior book layout, design, and using a professional cover artist/designer. Even so, it is becoming more difficult to find readers. If you liked this book, please leave a review and tell your friends. Those small actions help a lot.

Reviews may be left on the platform of your choice or emailed directly to me through my blog.

Thank you,

Eric Martell

Venice, 2021